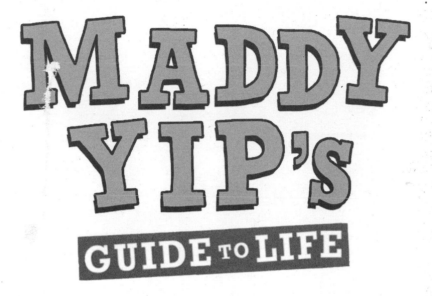

MADDY YIP'S

GUIDE TO LIFE

LOOK OUT FOR MORE IN THIS SERIES!

Maddy Yip's Guide to Holidays

MADDY YIP'S

GUIDE TO LIFE

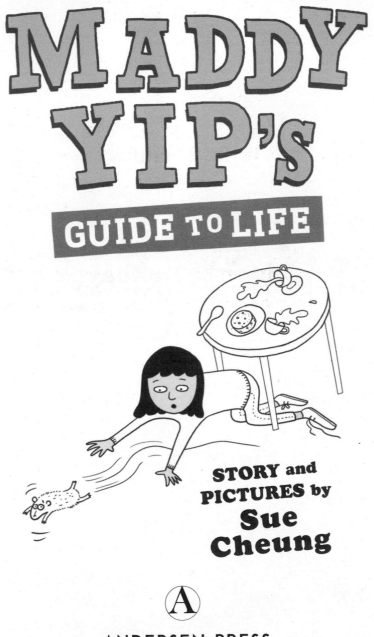

STORY and PICTURES by Sue Cheung

ANDERSEN PRESS

First published in 2021 by
Andersen Press Limited
20 Vauxhall Bridge Road, London SW1V 2SA, UK
Vijverlaan 48, 3062 HL, Rotterdam, Nederland
www.andersenpress.co.uk

2 4 6 8 10 9 7 5 3 1

British Library Cataloguing in Publication Data available.

ISBN 978 1 83913 049 6

Printed and bound in Great Britain by Clays Ltd,
Elcograf S.p.A.

To Dave,
whose talent is being married
to me and never losing his patience
(apart from the time I ironed
creases into his jeans).

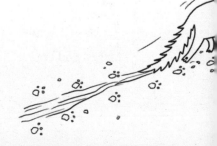

(DEV'S LITTLE SISTER)

TOOTY-
TOOOOOT-
TOOTY-
TOOOOOO
OOT!!!

Marginally
less annoying
than Oli

(DEV'S DOG)

WHOO-WHOO-
WHOOOOOOOOOO!!!

Marginally less
annoying than
Fuzzface

KAYLA DIGBY

No way is
Jack going
out with an
intellectual!

FLAMING
LYCHEEBILL

The most exciting
thing to happen to
Agung since instant
cup noodles

Saturday

UGH.

Weekends are officially ruined.

Mam was only meant to childmind the Tatlocks' twins during the week, but now they are coming on Saturdays too! Yesterday while I was at school, they sneaked into my room and painted a **stegosaurus** on the wall with ketchup. Then they wiped their dirty hands all over my favourite Kermit T-shirt. How can three-and-a-half year olds be so evil? Dad thought I was overreacting when I asked for a lock on my door. Just wait until they smear goo all over his pristine magnolia walls, we'll see who is crying then!

I planned a trip to the shop with Dev so I didn't have to be in when Ted and Tod (AKA **EVIL TWINS**) arrived. Dev is my best mate. We're both eleven but bonded at infant school after discovering our shared love of armpit farts. We were about to leave the house when Mr Tatlock came walking down the path with **EVIL TWINS**. He gave Mam a bag of toys, said thanks and left.

When me and Dev went to leave, Mam said, 'And where do you think you're going?!'

I said, 'To buy snacks.'

'No, you're not,' she said, 'the pipe's just burst under the sink and water's going everywhere, so you're looking after the twins while I fix it.'

WHAAAT?!

Don't like creepy-crawlies!

SPLAT!

But I wasn't qualified to be in charge of these . . . mini thugs! I've seen them smash ladybirds in with a hammer. Imagine what they could do to me. Dev said he didn't mind helping. He thinks the twins are 'entertaining'. He *would*. He goes to drama club where everybody loves a scene. I was about to argue back, but Mam was giving me that glare that can crack concrete a mile off, so I thought better of it. (She goes boxing at the gym and is hard as nails).

We took the twins into the back garden where Tod immediately picked up a plant pot and smashed it on the ground to smithereens.

BRILLIANT.

I grabbed them both and shoved them on their tricycles while we swept up the mess. The next thing we heard was Mr Pike shouting next door. We turned round and Ted was trying to chuck our cat over his fence. Mr Pike is a **GRUMPY CODGER** with a 'face like a chewed toffee' (Dad's words, not mine). He hates **FUZZFACE** and has threatened to take the law into his own hands if she ever uses his alpine rockery as a litter tray again.

I didn't want any trouble so I grabbed the hose and aimed it at Ted. 'Put the cat down and step away from the fence!' I told him, in my most authoritative voice. He didn't respond so I signalled to Dev to turn on the tap. It was only meant to be a light spray but the water came blasting out and knocked Ted off the bucket he was standing on. **FUZZFACE** *YOWLED* and pounced on Tod, who also fell over.

Then all three got up and ran into the house covered in mud.

'QUICK, DEV, STOP THEM!' I yelled, but it was too late.

Mam marched out, pointing at the house, **'HAVE YOU SEEN THE MESS IN THERE?!'**

Mr Pike looked pleased that we were in trouble. I turned the tap off sheepishly. Agung, my grandad, wandered out to see what was going on. He was dunking a coaster into a cup of tea thinking it was a biscuit. He is as blind as a bat without his glasses on.

Dev rubbed off some specks that had landed on his tie-dye leggings and tried to be helpful by saying to Mam, 'I've heard Sparklez Liquid's oxi formula is proven to remove a hundred per cent of stains.'

'Yeah, well get on with it then!' said Mam. 'This house needs a proper clean and you're all doing it now!' She pointed at me and said, 'There's still dried ketchup on your bedroom wall for a start.' Which I thought was unfair considering it was the twins that did it.

'And Jack can clean his petri dish of a room too!' she shouted up at his bedroom window.

The window opened and my big brother Jack shouted down at me aggressively. **'You owe me for this!'**

He is fourteen and trying to grow a moustache. He was probably mad at me because he'd planned to go to town to impress some girl with the three wispy chin hairs and monobrow he has managed so far.

Dev shuffled out of the side gate and sang out, **'See ya, wouldn't want to be ya!'**

So much for being a loyal friend.

While Mam cleaned up **EVIL TWINS** I had to clean the living room. It seemed like a relatively easy job until I saw the billion cat paw prints on every single surface. My arm was aching by the time I got to the cabinet. I am not cut out for manual labour. I am only four foot six. The cabinet is full of trophies and prizes. Oli, my little brother, has the most. One for swimming, one for football and one for hacky sack, whatever that is. I noticed he didn't have one for **Biggest Blabbermouth** though. He is excellent at that. Jack has two framed school certificates, Mam has a boxing medal and Agung has a

Best Exotic Vegetable rosette. Dad doesn't have a prize, he's got a silver tankard with a miniature schnauzer on that he hand-etched himself. He is dead creative.

It was then that I suddenly realised. All my family are good at something, **except me**! I tried to think if I had any talents. I did knit a scarf once. It never got finished so I gave it to Dad for Christmas as a bookmark.

I tried roller skating too, but could only go in one direction. Unfortunately that direction was straight into a gigantic bramble bush. It took Mam a whole day to tweeze the thorns out of my shins.

I was trying to think of more things, when Dad appeared with the hoover. 'I didn't realise the carpet was this colour underneath all this dirt,' he commented, surprised. He is not used to tidying. He is normally riffling through people's skips in his spare time and bringing back rubbish so he can make useful things out of them.

I went upstairs out of his way and scuttled past Jack's open door.

'Oi, Nut, come here!' he shouted.

UGH. I crept into his room.

'Yes?' I said.

'I was meant to be meeting mates in town. *Now* look at me!'

He was holding a pink feather duster, so I couldn't look at him (without laughing in his face). Nut, by the way, sounds like an affectionate term, but it's not. He calls me that because I once got a roasted peanut wedged up my nose when I was five. I nearly got taken to hospital but Dad threw pepper in my face and I sneezed it out. Jack thought it was so gross he has never let me forget about it since.

'You're not getting away with this,' he said.

'OK, I get the message,' I answered, holding my hands up.

I still wondered what I was good at so I asked Jack what he thought and he said, 'Shoving peanuts up your nose.'

GREAT.

Nobody had warned me that spring cleaning required effort! I had disinfected the skirting boards, removed cobwebs and even hoovered the curtains. I didn't go as far as sorting my socks into matching pairs though, **I will never be that dull**! While tidying, I found a miniature plastic trophy under the bed which had been forgotten about. I'd won it in a game of

. . . at Bella Brady's birthday party when I was six. It might have been a pretend trophy but it was evidence that **I WAS GOOD AT SOMETHING**! I thought about putting it in

the cabinet but worried if Jack found it he would probably ridicule me with yet another stupid nickname such as 'Donkey' or even worse . . . 'Ass'! I didn't throw it away. You never know when a miniature plastic trophy might come in useful one day.

How NOT to win Pin the Tail on the Donkey

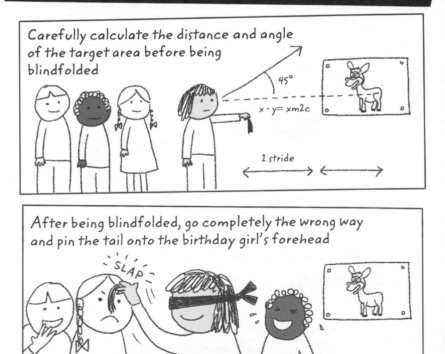

Maybe Oli knew what I might be good at. He was in our room too, cleaning. That's right, I have to **SHARE** a room with my seven-year-old brother. Dad put a 'divider curtain' across the middle. It hasn't helped. It just means that even though I am shielded from Oli's ugly mug, I can still hear him talking to **Luke Skywalker** (his action figure, not the actual greatest Jedi the galaxy has ever known).

'What do you think I'm good at?' I asked Oli.

'Ruining my life,' he sulked.

'Yeah, sorry about that,' I said, not sorry at all. 'Will you clean my half of the room if I give you a quid?' I asked.

16

'No.'

'Two quid?'

'**NO!**'

'Two quid and packet of pickled onion *CROCODILE CRUNCHIES*?'

'**MAAAAAAAMMMMM!!!!**'

God, little brothers **are such a pain.** I didn't want Mam going mad at me again so I went downstairs and hid in Agung's room. Agung is Dad's dad. He moved over from Hong Kong (glam) a few years ago and lives in the garage (not so glam). People might think that is cruel but the garage conversion is actually the best room in the house. It is massive and has a bed, sofa, telly and kettle. A total palace compared to my pathetic half-room hovel!

MASSIVE ROOM

'Sorry wrong answer. Baby aardvarks are actually called cubs...'

ALL TO HIMSELF!

Agung was watching a quiz show, which is **bonkers** because he can hardly speak English.

Apart from Dad who speaks Chinese, everyone else has to communicate with Agung by talking English in slow motion and doing terrible sign language.

Someone on the telly had won and was getting handed a trophy. Then I remembered the cabinet full of trophies and it made me feel depressed again . . .

I needed to find my talent or **I would forever be a loser**!

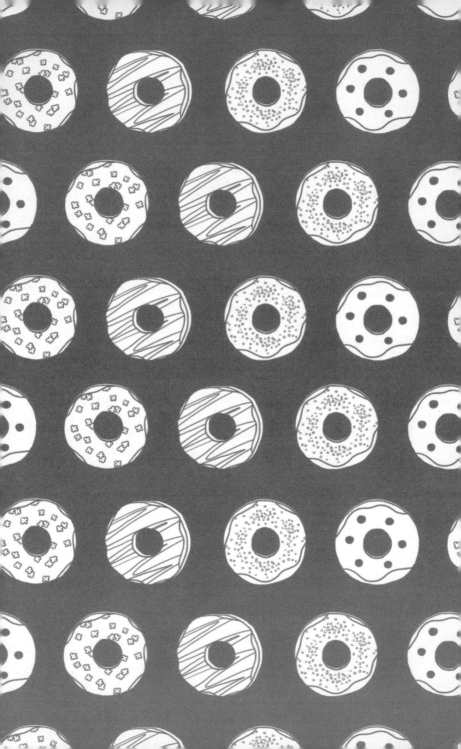

Sunday

I was still in bed the next morning when Dev came round to get me. He woke me up by pulling off the duvet and shouting, **'Get up, you're late for school!'** I almost had a heart attack. Then I realised it was Dev being a pillock . . . and it was Sunday.

'Come on, let's get chocolate!' he said. We never made it to the shops yesterday so snacks were overdue.

'Doughnut,' I grumbled,
pulling the duvet back on.

'Yeah, those too!' he replied.

The thought of **doughnuts** eventually got
me out of bed. I must have burned the equivalent
of twenty-five just folding my pants yesterday.
I got dressed and we headed off to the shop to
replenish the calories.

Afterwards we went back to Dev's house
where he has his own bedroom and no
annoying little brother. He has a five-year-
old sister called Heena, but she has her own
bedroom and is only mildly irritating. He has
a mongrel called Graham too who is just as
nuts as **FUZZFACE**. Unlike me, Dev has many

talents. One of them is turning his eyelids inside out, which is totally **VOMIT INDUCING**. The others are singing and dancing. He has two certificates hanging on his bedroom wall. One for Grade One singing and the other for tap dancing.

'I wish I was talented,' I said, having a closer look at his certificates. 'I had to clean our trophy cabinet yesterday. None of them were mine. I'm the untalented one of the family.'

'Don't be daft,' said Dev. 'Everyone has a talent. I bet I can find out what yours is.'

Well good luck to him, **HA**! I thought it would take him **AGES** but within seconds he had a brainwave. He chucked a bag of marshmallows at me and said, 'I know, let's see how many of these you can cram into your mouth at once!'

'I know, why don't you come back to me when you've thought of something less idiotic?' I answered.

Dev tapped his phone and showed me the screen. 'Look, the world record is fifty-one by a great-granny in Flemingsville, Kentucky, USA. You could beat that easy with your **massive gob**!'

I wasn't sure if that was a compliment or not.

Dev scrolled through his phone again, looking puzzled.

24

'But it doesn't say whether she had her teeth in.'

UGH.

I wasn't about to **humiliate myself** by trying to beat some toothless nonagenarian who lives in a place where they don't have anything better to do – plus what a waste of marshmallows! I racked my brain and remembered the plastic trophy that I'd found under the bed.

'I've got a better idea,' I said.

Dev didn't answer. He was too busy squashing a handful of marshmallows into his gob in an attempt to break the world record himself.

'I won a **Pin the Tail on the Donkey** game when I was six,' I said.

'Yeah, amph?' said Dev, shoving another in.

'So then I must be good at doing things with my eyes shut!'

'**Mmmph mmmamph mumph,**' Dev replied.

He was half suffocating and unable to interrupt so I took the opportunity to tell him about the trophy I got at **BELLA BRADY'S PARTY**. Dev responded by regurgitating pink, fluffy goo into the bin.

'If that's what you think then forget about it!' I said.

'No, that's a great idea,' said Dev. 'But how do we prove you're good at doing things with your eyes shut?'

There was only one way to find out. I grabbed a pencil and pad, got him to blindfold me and said, 'Ask me to draw something.'

'The cross section of a sixteenth-century galleon,' he replied.

Winding me up on purpose is another of Dev's many talents. I gave him my **'seriously?'** face.

'OK, a warthog then,' he said.

I have only set eyes on a warthog once. It was when Agung was watching a nature documentary about their social behaviour in savanna habitats. Basically they are just angry pigs with revolting body hair and oversized teeth. (Maybe Warthog could be my nickname for Jack. **HA! HA!**). I pictured one in my head and started scribbling, certain that the lines were going in all the right places. When I finished

I took off my blindfold to take in my accomplished masterpiece.

'It's got two heads,' Dev muttered.

"THEY HAVE A COMPLICATED BONE STRUCTURE!" I replied, throwing down my pencil in a strop. I was *sure* that was going to be my talent. How disappointing.

'Anyway, who gives prizes for drawing anatomically correct warthogs with their eyes shut?' Dev pointed out.

I was sorry to admit it, but he was right.

He brought the subject back to his drama club, which he has mentioned a **BILLION** times before. He has wanted me to join since I was five, even though he knows I can't sing, dance or act. I reminded him about the infant school nativity when I played a shepherd. Mary was handing me baby Jesus (a doll, I'll add at this point), and as I stepped forward the tea towel on my head slipped over my eyes and I *tripped* over a hay bale. Jesus went FLYING out of my arms and landed on Miss Wimple's (one of the dinner ladies) lap on the front row. She was so shocked she **jumped UP** and her bag of mint humbugs launched into the air like a fountain of hailstones. I went to retrieve Jesus but **slid** on a humbug, fell off the stage and **knocked** Miss Wimple flat on her backside. The whole place erupted with laughter and she

30

was utterly humiliated. She never did give me a full serving of chips after that.

'And that's what put me off drama ever since,' I said.

'Maybe comedy's more your thing then,' Dev replied, unhelpfully.

I didn't want to be a comedian. I wanted to be taken seriously for once. I went home feeling deflated and a **BIT SICK** after too many marshmallows. Unlike my warthog, Dad was sketching an actual masterpiece at the kitchen table, which made me feel even more nauseous.

'What's that?' I asked.

'I'm designing a bird table for Agung. Well, not for his own personal use, it'll be way too small!' he snorted, laughing at his own joke.

Then Agung walked in and said something to me in Chinese. I don't know why he does that because he knows full well I can hardly understand a word. Dad translated and said, 'There's been rare sightings of the Asian **Flaming Lycheebill** in the area, according to Agung's sources, and he's hoping this bird table will lure it in.' Agung's sources are his second cousins, the Chans, who run the **BAMBOO GARDEN** Chinese takeaway in the high street.

So Dad is going to build a bird table, probably made from bits of old scrap he finds in skips. It will end up looking like a work of art as usual. I will never be as good as him at anything. Or anyone else in the family for that matter.

TREMBLE

Monday

Mam made pancakes for breakfast. I thought it was a special occasion but I couldn't think what it was.

It wasn't my parents' anniversary, as Dad normally buys Mam an expensive bunch of flowers. Not because he is kind, generous and thoughtful, but because his mate at work's wife is a florist and can do him a good deal.

It was nobody's birthday either. It couldn't have been **FUZZFACE**'s or Hulk's. **FUZZFACE** was a stray that turned up in our hallway two years ago. Nobody ever claimed her. I am not surprised, she is out of control! Hulk is the ancient-looking school guinea pig that Oli is currently looking after. Despite his name, Hulk is not threatening in the least. He is the size of bellybutton fluff and could probably blow away in the wind. He used to live in a hutch in the classroom, but because of his nervous disposition he couldn't stand the screaming kids and his fur fell out. None of the other kids would go near him after that because he looked so

TREMBLE

36

weird. But Oli thought he resembled a **Star Wars** character called **Babu Frik**, so on that basis he volunteered to take him home.

It didn't matter what the occasion was, I was just looking forward to something other than cheapo, own brand Ricicle Krisps. Mam is going through a healthy-eating phase so she made the pancakes sugar-, gluten- and dairy-free. The excitement soon wore off when she told me that. I noticed Agung was using one of them as a tea coaster. He has a problem with coasters. And to be honest, it was probably the best use for it anyway.

'Thought you might need cheering up,' said Mam.

Pancakes that weren't sugar-, gluten- and dairy-free would have done the trick.

'You've been a bit glum lately, everything all right?' she added.

I lifted my chin off the table and sighed.

'It's just... **I'M NOT GOOD AT ANYTHING**!' I blurted. 'Everyone except me has got something in the trophy cabinet. **I'M A TOTAL LOSER**.'

Mam laughed as if I was making a big fuss over nothing. How would she like it if her highest achievement in life was winning a ridiculous party game?

'Don't be silly, you're clever at loads of things!' she said, all high-pitched.

'Like what?' I said, taking a slug of orange juice and spilling it all down my jumper.

'Well er, there's er . . .'

'ARMPIT FARTS!' shouted Oli.

'Shoving peanuts up your nose,' Jack added.

The world is a sad place when you have to live with brothers as immature as mine.

'You two, shut your traps!' said Mam, giving them the concrete-cracking glare.

She raised her eyebrows at Dad in a strange up and down way. I could almost hear the cogs grinding in his head as he thought long and hard of something. 'Oh, there was that time you won the **Pin the Tail on the Donkey** game!' he said.

Agung burped loudly.

'My thoughts exactly,' I commented back.

He chuckled and said something in Chinese.

The conversation came to an abrupt end after that. It was probably for the best as we would have been sitting there until nightfall thinking about what I was good at.

At school Dev was late for lunch which meant that Ged Sponger came and sat opposite me. I've never got on with him because quite frankly, he is the **biggest plonker in Plunkthorpe.**

Hold on . . . that means even Ged has a talent!

AMAZING.

I avoided eye contact with him by arranging the rice on my plate into the shape of a Teenage Mutant Ninja Turtle. A second later a spade-like hand reached across and tried to pull my plate away.

'You eatin' this?' Ged said, gruffly.

It was chilli con carne. I didn't want a reason

to make Ged mad so I warned him it was spicy.

'Eugh,' he growled, pushing it back. 'Next time, get something I can eat.'

HA! Anyone would think I was Ged's humble servant or something!

Dev (literally) waltzed in a moment later.

'Where have you been?' I said, annoyed at being left with Ged, the medieval tyrant.

'It's a surprise,' he replied.

I hate surprises. Unless it involves snacks, spending money or evidence that unicorns exist.

'Listen,' he went on, 'about the talent thing. I have an idea!'

Dev reckons everyone is good at something if they look hard enough. It's all right for him, he was born multi-talented, while I sing like a **strangled crow** and dance like I'm being **ELECTROCUTED** on an ice-rink. Also, his sole ambition in life is to own a **CRYSTAL-STUDDED** jumpsuit and star in an award-winning Broadway musical, while mine is just to get through the day without stepping in dog muck.

'What you need . . .' he announced, flouncing his arms in a big arch.

I braced myself for another one of his madcap plans.

'. . . is a **MENTOR**.'

'What, like a teacher?' I said, confused.

'Yeah, but a teacher of **talent**,' Dev replied. 'I've got the skills to transform you into one of Plunkthorpe's finest legends.'

Not exactly Broadway, but beggars can't be choosers.

'OK, so you want to be my mentor, fine,' I said.

Anything to get a proper trophy of my own in the cabinet.

'Awesomesauceness!' said Dev, clutching his palms to his chest. 'I'll do some research and get back to you with ideas, pronto. Oh, and this is the surprise.'

He reached into his rucksack and pulled out something *gold* and *sequinned*. I was almost blinded by the dinner hall's fluorescent lights reflecting off it.

'What's that?' I asked.

'This is the lucky waistcoat I wore when I got my certificates for singing and tap dancing. I don't need it now I'm on a certain path to **STARDOM**, so I'm passing its magical powers on to you.'

Dev doesn't half talk a load of baloney. But I must say after my eyes adjusted, the waistcoat did have a certain enchanting quality to it. Mind you, even a wooden spoon would seem enchanting after sitting next to Ged Sponger for half an hour. Then I remembered I had a slight phobia of waistcoats, ever since Mam made me wear one for Aunt Tanya's engagement party when I was four. I'd eaten a plate full of sausage rolls and was sick down the front of it. Mam cleaned it up but you can see the stain in all the photos – so humiliating.

Caught in the act!

Needing emergency sick bucket
(Jack not impressed)

Obvious stainage

'You can be my mentor, but I am **NOT** wearing that thing,' I said.

Dev sniffed it and replied, 'Hmm, it smells of boiled onions anyway.'

CHARMING.

Jack gave me the evil eye all evening. He still hasn't forgiven me for making him miss out on going to town with his mates on Saturday. As far as I'm concerned I did him a favour because while cleaning he found **Ninja Banana 2** stuck behind the radiator. He has been looking for that video game for six months. Also there was a mug under his bed that Dad had to retrieve with a pair of barbeque tongs and chuck straight into the outside bin. It was full of furry, blue mould. I have saved Jack from contracting a deadly bacterial disease and get no thanks in return. **Typical!** His silent treatment made me uncomfortable so I went to my room. Oli was in there making **Luke Skywalker** fight Hulk with one of Agung's chopsticks in the absence of a lightsaber.

I reminded Oli to go gentle on Hulk, he wouldn't want him turning bald again. (Hulk has grown back all his fur since leaving the bedlam of the classroom.)

I wonder what Dev has in store for me. It is making me nervous.

Friday

Dad has been in the shed every night this week making Agung's bird table. During the day he is a warehouse manager at a car metal parts factory. He finds it agonisingly dull, apart from Fridays, when there's Toad in the Hole in the canteen. His **dream** is to come up with an invention that will make enough money to buy a house where Agung isn't stuck in the garage and so Dad can retire and rummage through even more skips.

Mam thinks bringing back other people's rubbish is unhygienic. She never complains when he's turned it into something useful, though. The saucepan rack he made gets shown off to everyone who comes round, including the electricity meter man. I am sure he is more interested in finishing his rounds than listening to her harp on about effective storage solutions. (Must look into whether saucepan racks could be a money spinner).

How to make money-spinning inventions

Dad's pan rack (basically a towel holder and some hooks)

Invisible elastic that keeps shoes together (so Agung can always wear a matching pair)

Portable pedestrian crossing so you can safely cross the road wherever and whenever

Anti Bully Spray

Repel bullies with the wholesome smell of 'NICENESS' !!!

Dev's been asking me all sorts of questions to help with his research. After school he asked if I was psychic and I replied, 'Well if I was, I'd know what my flippin' **talent** was, wouldn't I?!' While he was off thinking up more daft questions I asked Dad if I could help with the bird table. You never know, there could be the minutest chance that I had inherited his craft skills. I was surprised he said yes, as he knows how clumsy I can be. Just this morning I fell **UP** the stairs. The carpet burn is still visible under my chin. By all accounts 'falling up' shouldn't be possible. Jack, who is a science geek, said it defied the laws of gravity. I wondered if that counts as a talent? I should check the Guinness World Records.

'I'm off to the **BAMBOO GARDEN** with Agung to get us Chinese takeaway for tea,' Dad said.

'Can you finish off the bird table with a lick of paint all over?'

HA! DID HE THINK I WAS A TOTAL DIMWIT? Anyone is capable of slopping on a bit of paint.

'Never fear, Dad, you're looking at the next Michelangelo,' I assured him.

'Well as long as you're not the next Jackson Pollock, that's all right,' he replied, shoving a brush and tin of paint in my hands and walking off.

I didn't know who Jackson Pollock was but I'm sure he wasn't as bad as Dad made out. The bird table looked superb. It was like a miniature

Swiss cottage on a stick. I felt honoured to be contributing to Dad's fine piece of craftmanship. I prised open the paint tin lid with the screwdriver and was shocked to see the colour inside. It was **luminous orange**! Maybe Dad has been colour blind all along and I wasn't aware? Or maybe he wanted to help birds locate the table in the dark? Anyway I was sure Dad knew what he was doing, so I laid some old newspaper on the lawn and made a start. I was onto the roof part when I stopped to rest my eyes. The glare of the paint was burning into my retinas. I looked up and spotted **FUZZFACE** about to attack a pigeon. All I could think was there'd be a massive scuffle and a million feathers would get stuck to my freshly painted bird table, so I panicked and shouted **'NO!'**

The pigeon got startled and flew towards me. It might as well have been a pterodactyl, it was so squawky and terrifying! I backed off and knocked over the paint tin and cringed as a huge, orange lake spilled across the newspaper and onto the lawn. Then I winced while **FUZZFACE** trotted through it dragging her bushy tail behind her as she followed the pigeon into Mr Pike's garden through a gap in the fence.

I crept up to the fence and peeked over it.

ARRRRGGGGH!

Mr Pike's decking was spattered in luminous paw prints and tail stripes. I covered my eyes to make it all go away but when I uncovered them, all I could see was Mr Pike at his dining-room window, open mouthed in disbelief. **Oh no, I was in trouble now.**

Just then Dad came out to tell us tea was ready. He nearly had a fit when he saw the paint spillage in our garden. Then he had an actual one when he noticed the bird table.

'**WHY IS THE BIRD TABLE LUMINOUS ORANGE?!**' he screamed, almost like a girl.

'That's the colour you gave me,' I muttered.

He went over and picked up the paint tin.

'But it says "Chestnut Brown" on here!'

'Not another one of your skip finds was it?'
tutted Mam, who had come out to see what Dad
was yelling about.

Then Mr Pike came out of his house, ranting,
'Have you seen this?!'

'It's impossible not to!' said Dad.

**'No, not your garden,
MINE!'** Mr Pike bellowed, pointing at
his decking.

Dad looked over the fence. **FUZZFACE** stopped licking her tail, stared at Dad and meowed.

'JACKSON POLLOCK!!!' Dad shouted, eyes bulging. 'I mean, sorry Mr Pike, I'll come over immediately with the paint remover.'

Mr Pike went back inside, fuming. I hoped he wasn't going to call the police. While Dad was cleaning up Mr Pike's decking, Mam had to put **FUZZFACE** in a tub and scrub her with a whole bottle of Sparklez Liquid. The paint wouldn't come off in places so she had to cut those bits off. Afterwards **FUZZFACE** looked very undignified with chunks missing from her fur and had a sad expression on her face for ages. Serves her right for being a delinquent.

I guess Dad won't be leaving me in charge of his projects any more. He doesn't need a repeat of this to remind him how clumsy I am. Although he did admit the paint colour was entirely his fault, he made me tidy the shed as punishment. While I was sifting through the storage chest, I found a wooden box with a slide-off top and bottom. Dad said it was a magic box that he had made ages ago. He wanted to bin it but I wanted to find out how it worked, so I kept it.

Jack collared me on the landing after dinner and told me to help him with something tomorrow. He is doing experiments for his school science project. I hope it won't involve throwing blazing knives at me, or sitting in a bath full of worms. It seems I don't have much choice in the matter as I still 'owe' him for the cleaning incident.

Saturday

Was at Dev's again this morning. Mam thinks I am doing homework but really I am doing something more important and staying well away from **EVIL TWINS**. Especially today as Mam was planning on making playdough with them out of flour, water and food colouring. I dread to think of the resulting carnage! Mr Tatlock doesn't pick them up until one o'clock so Mrs Sharma (Dev's mam) insisted I stay for a delicious Indian lunch.

This was an added bonus as Mam is still cooking disgusting health food.

Dev was wearing a psychedelic kaftan. He found it in a charity shop in town. I asked which one and he said Age Concern. More like Fashion Concern, if you ask me. I told Dev about the **paint pandemonium** and he was gutted he'd missed it. Then I showed him the box I'd found in the shed. 'We've got one of those at drama club,' he said. 'They're magic.' It would be magic if Dev ever got round to revealing his mentoring plans. Whenever I ask he taps the side of his nose and says, 'All good things come to those who wait.' I've been waiting for my own bedroom since birth and that hasn't happened yet, so that saying can't be true.

When Dev went to the loo I had a nose around his desk. There was a yellow notepad on it with 'M.M.M.' written on the cover in metallic purple pen. When I looked inside I saw that the 'M.M.M.' stood for 'MENTORING MADDY TO MEGASTARDOM'. At last! I could see what he was up to! He had only filled in one page which read:

PLAN OF ACTION

- BUY THIS PAD ✓
- BUY THIS METALLIC PURPLE PEN ✓
- DO RESEARCH
- TRANSFORM MADDY INTO ONE OF PLUNKTHORPE'S FINEST LEGENDS

WHAAAT?!

He had only got as far as acquiring a writing implement! I quickly put the pad down when I heard him coming back. I was disappointed that in five days, that was all he'd managed. I couldn't blame him though. I did warn him I wasn't good at anything.

When I got home, Jack was carrying a box down the stairs. 'Hey, Nut, take this to the garden!' he ordered, thrusting it at me. He is becoming very bossy these days. Dad says it's **teenage hormones**, but I reckon he's annoyed that his moustache hasn't made an appearance yet. 'It's the experiments you need to help me with,' he said. I was still worried about what he wanted me to do, then remembered I was searching for my hidden talent and had to be up for trying anything at this stage, even if it did mean sitting in a **bath full of worms**. I needn't have worried though as the box only had pop bottles, plasticine, coloured card, and a tube of chewy mints in it. Jack told me the three experiments would be:

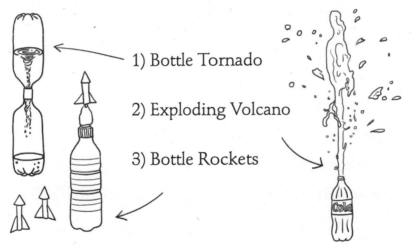

1) Bottle Tornado

2) Exploding Volcano

3) Bottle Rockets

They sounded quite dangerous. It was too late to back out though. I would just have to be prepared for a visit to A&E. It turned out my job was fairly simple in the end. For the first experiment Jack filled an empty bottle three quarters full of water, then added a few drops of washing up liquid and a sprinkle of glitter. All I had to do was tip the water from one bottle to the other until a mini tornado formed inside. I couldn't believe it, my **scientific talents** were unfolding before my very eyes! Jack jotted down some notes then set up the Exploding Volcano. This required a two-litre bottle of cola and a tube of mints. I had to take the mints out of the pack and Sellotape them back together in a strip, which I thought was **strange**. I quite like mints so I ate a few while I was doing it. OK, maybe half the pack. When Jack saw me he went **mad**. Hearing him, Mam ran out into the garden and when she saw what we were doing she said,

'**No way are you doing that here!**' She pointed at our washing hanging on the line. 'Lorraine's kids did this . . . "volcano" thing the other day and it wrecked her valance!'

I had no idea what a valance was but I hoped Lorraine didn't have to go to the doctor's about it. 'Sling your hook!' said Mam, pointing vaguely into the far distance.

We decided to go to the park. There was no danger of wrecking anything there, unless any poor, unsuspecting squirrels got in the way. Jack made me stop off at the shop for another packet of mints while he went to unload the box in the park. How was I to know I wasn't supposed to eat the experiment? It should have been in the instructions!

On the way out of the shop I bumped into Ged Sponger lumbering past.

UGH.

He asked what I'd just bought.

'Nowt,' I said, sliding the sweets up my sleeve.

I wondered what was worse, Ged nicking the mints or Jack going mad at me for failing as his assistant again. I had to live with Jack (worst luck!), so it was better to stay in his good books.

I didn't have any better defence so I just ran away as fast as I could. It seemed to do the trick as Ged was nowhere to be seen when I reached the park. (Probably he decided to save his energy to plot his next assault on me).

I gave Jack the mints and this time *he* taped them up. '**Right, now get out of the way!**' he shouted, unscrewing the bottle lid. I'd been bossed around by Jack all day and wasn't about to miss a good, close-up view just because he said so. I ignored his advice and watched as he dropped the mints through the top of the bottle and sprinted away as fast as he could. Within a nanosecond the cola came spraying out in a massive six-foot fountain and ended up completely drenching me.

71

GREAT.

'Hahahaha! You nut, Nut!' laughed Jack, doubled up. 'I told you to move!'

I wanted to go home and change my clothes but Jack wouldn't let me. It was my job to do the **Bottle Rockets** experiment while he took photos. I could feel a rash coming up so I decided to get it over and done with as quickly as possible. I inserted one of the rockets onto the end of an empty bottle and squeezed as hard as I could. I wasn't paying attention and the rocket **shot up** and got stuck in a tree. Jack told me to concentrate but it is difficult when you're itching in strange places.

The next two rockets got stuck in the tree too and this time Jack was **livid** because he needed to take them to school to show his science teacher. He ordered me to go up and retrieve them but by then the cola had **practically glued** my eyelashes together and I could hardly see a thing.

In the end Jack lost his patience and went up the tree himself. He had his brand new, white trainers on so he was **fuming**. He nearly fell twice trying not to mark them.

Just then Kayla Digby walked by. I knew who she was because she hangs around with the popular brainy girls at school. She was looking worried and calling out,

'Munchikins, Munchikins!'

She looked up and saw Jack, who went red in the face. He almost fell out of the tree again trying to rearrange his hair into an attractive style. I suspected she was the secret girl he'd been trying to impress for ages.

74

Then we heard a tiny 'meow'. Jack parted some leaves and found a kitten stuck on a low branch.

'Oh!' Kayla swooned. 'You've found my fluffy Munchikins, what a hero!'

(I could not believe someone would give their cat that name).

Jack laughed nervously and opened his mouth but nothing came out. How embarrassing. I coughed. 'Yeah,' I said. 'We heard meowing so Jack, being brave and all that, decided to go and rescue your kitten.'

'You're in my year, aren't you?' Kayla asked Jack.

'Heh, heh, yeah,' was all Jack could muster. He really wasn't helping himself.

He brought the kitten down, scuffing his immaculate trainers all the way, and gave it to Kayla. She asked Jack if he wanted to join her book club. He said yes and she told him her number while he typed it, all flustered, into his phone.

'Text me and I'll send you the details,' she said, taking the kitten's paw with her hand and making it wave.

YUCK.

Jack told her he liked history books. **HA!** The only history book he has ever read is *The Ultimate History of Video Games* – **WHAT A DORK!**

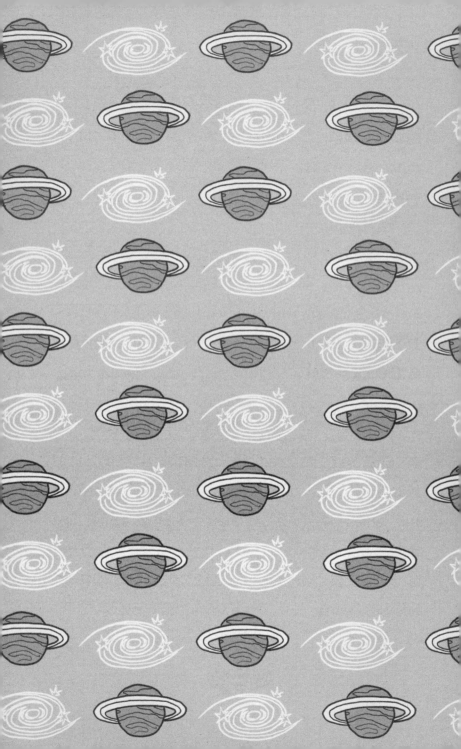

Saturday - a week later

Dad has put up the bird table. It is in Agung's bit of the garden at the back where he grows his veg. It is so luminous that astronauts can probably see it from the International Space Station without the aid of a telescope. During breakfast, we heard a commotion. We looked out of the kitchen window to see **FUZZFACE** jumping up at the sparrows feeding on the table. Dad went outside to go and stop her but was too late. **FUZZFACE** leaped on the roof and teetered for a second before toppling the whole thing over. Agung cried **'NOOOOO!'** as it landed in a whirlwind of feathers and leaves. Agung's eyesight was suddenly crystal clear when he saw his polytunnel being flattened. Dad said the table had to go as he couldn't allow our savage of a cat to use it as a death trap for birds. Dad is an environmentalist. He doesn't even like it when Mam rinses spiders down the plughole. Good job he's never around to see how **EVIL TWINS** treat wildlife!

I couldn't hide at Dev's this weekend because his family were away visiting relatives. I was given the job of feeding the Sharmas' dog Graham while they were out. Dad was with Agung at the Chans' and Jack was at book club, which meant that me and Oli were stuck in the house with **EVIL TWINS** for four hours.

HIDEOUS!

I hardly recognised them when they arrived. Usually they look as if they've crawled out of a sewer. Today they were dressed in their best clothes and their hair was combed into neat side partings. You could easily have been 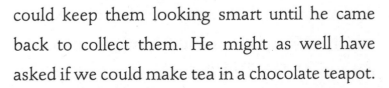 fooled into thinking they were innocent, angelic choir boys, but I saw through their disguise! They were going to a birthday party straight after ours. Mr Tatlock asked if we could keep them looking smart until he came back to collect them. He might as well have asked if we could make tea in a chocolate teapot.

Mam tried to think of something they could do that wouldn't end up in scraping gunk off the furniture. While she went to fetch the building bricks from the living room Oli started crying because Tod shoved his **Luke Skywalker** action figure down the toilet. Mam got her washing up gloves on and tried to remove him, but Luke was wedged tight. She pulled too hard on his arm and his hand snapped off, which made Oli cry even more. To calm him down, Mam told him she would replace it with the latest model which has realistic suede hair and moving eyes. This cheered him up no end. Ted came to the door and had a good gawp at what was going on – so evil. Mam was worried that the toilet would be blocked so she told me and Oli to take the twins into the living room and keep them there until she'd fixed the problem.

I ushered the twins into the living room and randomly pressed buttons on the telly remote until I found the kid's channel which did the job of shutting them up, so it was nice and peaceful for a change. When I looked at the time it was half past eleven! I'd been so preoccupied I'd forgotten to go and feed Graham.

'Oli, keep an eye on them while I give Graham his grub,' I said, jabbing a warning finger at EVIL TWINS.

'NO, DON'T LEAVE ME ON MY OWN!'

he whimpered, clutching my leg.

The twins were transfixed by the telly.

'Don't worry, *Wally the Walrus* will keep them occupied for hours,' I replied.

I was only out for a few minutes but when I returned I was **SHOCKED** to find that Oli and the twins had disappeared from the living room. I found them in the back garden, playing football. It looked fairly tame so it was all right. Oli was in goal while the twins tried to tap the ball in. There was no running around or falling over so I let them carry on. I don't know what Mam goes on about when she says childminding is a hard job. Sitting on a deckchair reading my comic while vaguely supervising from the sidelines was as easy as pie! I was a natural with kids. Maybe childminding was my hidden **talent**?

After a while, Ted came running over and complained about being hot. Even though the twins are identical I knew it was Ted because he always has **GREEN SNOT** oozing out of his right nostril. He wanted to take off his jumper but we were under strict orders to keep the twins looking the same as when they arrived so I went and got my handheld fan. I probably shouldn't have left him unattended with it because the next thing I knew he had got his fringe stuck in the whirring blades and completely snarled it up.

'Ow! Ow! Stuck!' Ted squealed, flapping his arms around like a demented gibbon.

'OK, hold still,' I replied, trying to act like a responsible adult in the absence of an actual responsible adult. I switched off the fan and hoped to God Mam was still busy wrestling **Luke Skywalker** out of the U-bend.

Just then Graham appeared from nowhere, barking like mad. I had left him in the Sharmas' garden to finish his bowl of Chompy Chunks.

This is NOT happening!

AAAAAGGHH!

He must have been lonely and decided to join in when he heard us having 'fun'. Graham is only a little mongrel but had managed to jump his fence, run across Mr Pike's garden and jump over our fence. I was still untangling Ted's hair when Graham whizzed over to Tod, who had the ball, and knocked him straight into the compost heap!

I closed my eyes, hoping it was all a dream, then opened them in time to see Graham burst the ball with his teeth.

EXCELLENT.

Oli started crying again. It was his best ball. Then Ted and Tod started blubbing too, and to top it all off, Graham started **howling**. I wasn't surprised when Mam came out with a face like thunder. It was then I decided that childminding was not a talent of mine.

'WHAT THE HECK?!' she cried, surveying the scene of utter chaos. 'I leave you alone for TWO seconds . . .!' (Mam has a habit of exaggerating when she gets mad).

I explained what had happened but it didn't help the fact that the twins were a **mess** and Mr Tatlock was due back any second.

Mam cut a wedge out of Ted's fringe to free the fan. It ended up **lopsided** so she trimmed the rest shorter to match. Ted didn't look evil after that, he just looked like an abandoned orphan. Mam didn't have time to wash Tod's smelly jumper either so she gave him my old waistcoat to wear instead. Mam swore it was clean but I could still detect a **HINT OF SICK** down the front of it from when I ate all those sausage rolls at Aunt Tanya's engagement party.

Weirdly Mr Tatlock didn't bat an eyelid when he came to collect **EVIL TWINS**. Dad says it is very stressful being a solicitor and that is why

89

Mr Tatlock walks around in a daze most of the time. I am a hundred per cent sure the daze is not caused by work-related stress but by having ferals for sons.

Jack had a stupid grin on his face all through dinner. He had been to Kayla's book club reviewing a local author's debut at the Owl's Den bookshop. She will soon go off him when his moustache makes *its* debut.

Agung complained about having a bad foot. When Dad offered to take a look Agung said not to worry as he had rubbed a piece of fresh ginger onto it. Apparently, it is a traditional Chinese remedy. Agung told Dad he had put the ginger back in the fridge where he'd found it. We nearly choked when we realised Dad had then put the ginger in the stir fry we were eating. None of us could finish eating after that, apart from Agung, who quite happily claimed our leftovers. Dad told Agung he can't go round rubbing our dinner on his ailments and will make an appointment for him to see the doctor.

How to attend to a medical complaint

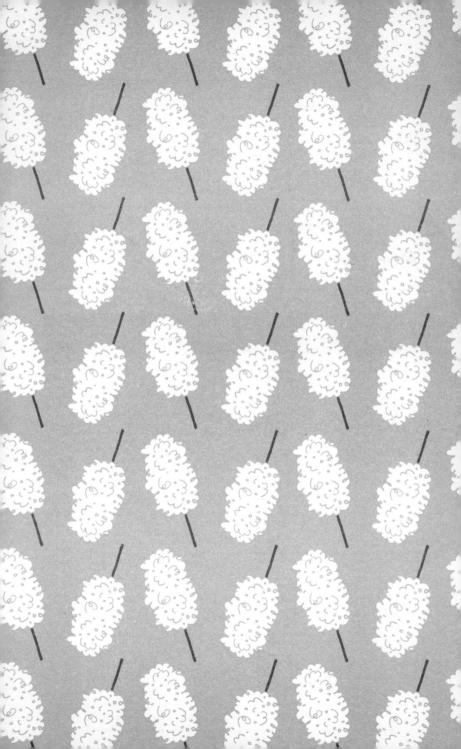

Monday

I wanted to ask Dev what progress he was making on my mentoring plans. So far, I had crossed painting, science and childminding off my **'Things I'm Potentially Ace At'** list. I was hoping he had some other suggestions before I resorted to sticking my head in a cupboard and repeatedly banging the door on it.

At morning break Dev came running over, upset. He tried to tell me what was wrong but

I couldn't understand a word because he was wheezing so badly. He had only jogged from the Design and Technology block twelve yards away. Dev is prone to asthma in **muggy weather**, plus he had non-regulation espadrilles on, which I'm sure don't offer any kind of foot support. I even had time to count the coins in my pocket and watch a seagull attack Matilda Ogden's cheese and onion pasty before he got his breath back.

'It's my drama club,' he gasped. **'It's closing down due to lack of funds!'**

He got his inhaler out and puffed on it.

I was shocked. The drama club has been Dev's second home for years. Just as his home has been my second home on Saturdays while hiding from **EVIL TWINS**. If the club shuts then Dev's certain path to stardom will be over with. 'What about other clubs?' I asked.

'But I don't like judo, macramé or political debate,' he said.

'No, drama clubs, you plum!'

'Well the next closest is High Heath, where the **POSH KIDS** go. All they do is Shakespeare which I don't get. Plus wearing an Elizabethan ruff makes my face look like a beach ball.'

Dev thinks his face is too round, but I tell him it's just puppy fat and he will grow out of it.

'And it's a half mile hike up a hill to get there,' he wailed. 'I can't do that with my lungs.'

He puffed on his inhaler again and his eyes welled up. I didn't know if he was about to sob or if he'd inhaled a bit too strenuously.

I have only ever known Dev to cry twice. Once when his SpongeBob SquarePants balloon burst and the other when an alpaca ate his candy floss at the Blogworth Agricultural Show.

I rooted about in my bag and gave him a tissue. It had a partially sucked boiled sweet stuck to it but Dev was in such a state of despair, he wouldn't have noticed. I felt I needed to help somehow. After all, he offered to help mentor me (even though there had been zero evidence of it so far).

Just before lunchtime, I had a brilliant idea and couldn't wait to tell him. 'Hey, Dev, I know how to save your drama club!' I said, as we queued for food.

'How?' he grumbled.

'Why don't you get all the members together and organise a variety show to raise money?'

Dev's eyes lit up and his mouth gaped open. 'Oh my God, why didn't I think of that? That's the best idea since the twenty-pee thing!'

Last April Fool's day I glued a twenty pence piece to the pavement outside Ged's house, then me and Dev both watched from behind a hedge while he tried to prise it off with a rubber spatula. It was the best laugh we've had in ages. I didn't think I could top that idea but what can I say, I am a highly imaginative individual.

We spent the rest of lunch discussing how to organise the show then at the end Dev grabbed my arm and said, **'I've got another idea!'**

I didn't like his tone of voice.

'YOU should perform as well!'

'I'd rather rub a lemon slice into my eyeball,' I scoffed.

Dev sifted through his rucksack and pulled out a familiar-looking yellow notepad. It was his **'MENTORING MADDY TO MEGASTARDOM'** notes.

'Take a look at this,' he said.

He slid it across the table in a mysterious manner. I pretended to be surprised. I didn't want to say I'd already flicked through it and was majorly disappointed. But this time, when I opened the pad it was full of scribbles and sketches.

On the last page it read:

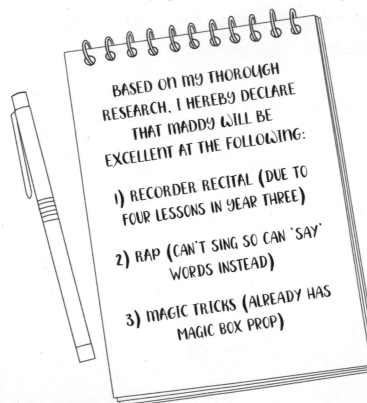

BASED ON MY THOROUGH RESEARCH, I HEREBY DECLARE THAT MADDY WILL BE EXCELLENT AT THE FOLLOWING:

1) RECORDER RECITAL (DUE TO FOUR LESSONS IN YEAR THREE)

2) RAP (CAN'T SING SO CAN 'SAY' WORDS INSTEAD)

3) MAGIC TRICKS (ALREADY HAS MAGIC BOX PROP)

UGH.

I was at least expecting tight-rope walking over a crocodile swamp or playing a spinet harpsichord. Recorder recital? That was kiddy stuff! If this was all Dev could come up with then I really was a **HOPELESS CASE**. I couldn't argue though, he'd had a tough job.

'What do you think?' said Dev.

'Amazing,' I lied.

After school we went round to Dev's drama club. We told Miss Gabb the club manager about our variety performance idea. She got so excited she grabbed a clown car horn from the prop basket,

parped it in my ear and half deafened me.
'WELL DONE, FANTASTIC IDEA! And
it'll be an ABSOLUTE BLAST!' she said,
pointing at the horn. She should get together
with Dad and form a bad joke appreciation
society. 'I'll start organising immediately.'

We went back to Dev's and he put me straight
to work with recorder practice, which I wasn't
really looking forward to.

'Slight problem,' I said, trying to sound bothered. 'I chucked my recorder in a ditch after I couldn't get the hang of "Amazing Grace".'

I was hoping to get away with it when Dev thought for a moment and replied, 'Problem solved. Heena's got one.'

FANTASTIC.

We found Heena in her Wendy House in the garden. She made us wait five minutes while she finished serving a pretend pork pie to Graham. I asked if we could borrow her recorder. She didn't want to at first as she was worried about germs. I pointed out that she should be more worried about Graham, who was sat there licking his bits then licking the plate with the invisible pork pie on it.

When I blew into the recorder it reminded me why I gave up in the first place, because no matter what note I tried to play they all sounded like somebody accidentally **treading on an owl** with a clog.

The rapping fared a little better as all I had to do was lip-synch. Opening and closing my mouth without a sound was easy. There was no time to write a rap from scratch so we asked Mr Sharma if he knew any good, classic songs we could use. 'Does a bear poop in the woods?' he replied. He scratched his head for ages then only managed to reel off three songs. We also had to stop him from searching in the attic for his old nineties tracksuit that he used to go to **HIP-HOP GIGS** in as a student.

'If you really want to look the part, you need to learn some **BREAKDANCING** moves, like the **WINDMILL**,' Mr Sharma suggested. He lay on the carpet and tried to demonstrate. From what I could see, it required rolling around on the floor like an upturned tortoise.

'It works better on a shiny floor,' he mumbled, tied up in a messy knot.

I thought **HIP HOP** was supposed to be cool. That didn't seem cool to me. Mrs Sharma walked in just as he did a pathetic backward roll. 'For goodness' sake, Amit, nobody wants to see your full moon bottom! Grow up and help me peel the potatoes.' Then she pushed Mr Sharma out of the door.

We wondered if the **WINDMILL** really would be better on a shiny floor so Heena let us borrow the square of lino from her Wendy House to try. When we went to get it, we found Graham asleep inside, presumably stuffed from all that non-existent party food he'd had earlier. We left the door open so he wouldn't wake up trapped among the nightmarish pink decor. After a few spins on the lino, I got a bruise on my right hip and had to call it day. I am not built for physical endurance, I am under the national average for my height.

'Let's see how this gizmo works then,' said Dev, handing me the **MAGIC BOX** I found in Dad's shed.

'I thought you said you had one of these at drama club?'

'Yeah, but I never said I knew what to do with it,' he answered, shrugging.

We both stared at it for a million hours as if the **MAGIC BOX** would give us a magic answer, then Dev said, 'Let's look online.' Which is what we should have done a million hours ago because the Internet is the secret to everything in life.

How to work the 'magic box'

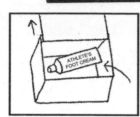

Slide open top lid. Put object in box.

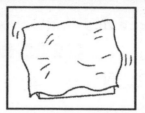

Replace lid. Cover box with cloth.

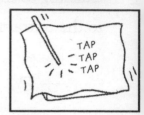

Do magical stuff with wand (or chopstick).

Slide off false bottom under cloth. Object falls out into hands.

Hide object elsewhere. Replace false bottom. Whip cloth away.

Open top lid to reveal object has mysteriously disappeared!

It was quite easy once we read the instructions. I succeeded in making a trainer, a radio alarm clock and a tube of athlete's foot cream disappear. However, I do need to work out how to use the slide-off bottom on the box properly. Once I can stop the items visibly crashing to the floor, it will look very convincing to the untrained eye.

After **EVIL TWINS** leave on Saturday, I will perform all three acts in front of Jack, Oli and Agung. They will mark me out of five for each one, then I will perform the winning act at the variety show.

Dad had taken Agung to the doctor's today about his sore foot. When I asked what the problem was Dad replied, 'He had **Luke Skywalker**'s hand wedged in his slipper.'

Saturday

On the day of judging Dev wanted me to wear a **LEOPARD SKIN TASSELLED ONESIE** he'd found at the back of his wardrobe. I refused on the grounds that it was horrendous. He is definitely not talented when it comes to picking tasteful clothing.

I purposely didn't ask the parents to judge. They'd have said everything I did was brilliant just to spare my feelings. On the other hand, Jack and Oli don't give a jot about my feelings.

They are **heartless buffoons**. Agung is only judging because we are using his room and he has no other choice. I must remember to make sure he is wearing his specs. The other day he went for a walk and Mrs Sharma had to bring him back because she found him throwing tea coasters (thinking they were biscuits) at a couple of logs floating in the park pond (thinking they were ducks). It is a good job the local constabulary didn't spot him. He could have been prosecuted for hooliganism!

After EVIL TWINS left, me and Dev set up in Agung's room. It wasn't ideal as it was full of junk and joss stick fumes that make your eyes water. We made space by pushing the sofa and coffee table to one side. Jack and Agung sat on the sofa.

Jack is a different person since going to Kayla's book club. He is bossing me about less, for a start. I like everything about the new Jack, apart from his cravat. It's supposed to make him look **intellectual** but just looks like he's forgotten to take his napkin off from dinner.

Agung did have his specs on but still managed to put a tartan slipper on one foot and a flip flop on the other. Oli ran whooping into the room.

'Someone's excited to see the show!' said Dev.

'No,' said Oli. 'I'm just glad to be free.' He had also been hiding from **EVIL TWINS** all morning.

As soon as everyone was settled, I started the recorder recital. It was 'When the Saints Go Marching In'. I played as loudly as I could and added a dance routine with a leg flick to either side. Oli asked if I had cramp so I stopped doing that. As I got to the second verse, we heard Graham howling from two doors down. Then one by one all the other neighbourhood dogs started joining in. Jack said that dogs can hear ultra-high notes

WHOO-WHOO-WHOOOOOOOOOOO!!!

114

that can't be detected by human ears. It was probably freaking them out.

'Dunno about the dogs but I'm freaking out here!' said Oli, sticking his fingers in his ears.

I tried to be professional by playing on, until we heard Mr Pike shout out,

'SHUT THAT BLEEDIN' RACKET!'

Dev told me it might be a good idea to stop before we got reported to the local authorities for noise disturbance. I was devastated about not finishing all seventeen verses – all that practice for nothing! Anyway, I did my best but the marks weren't great:

Oli = 1 ('It hurt my ears')

Agung = an upside down 2

Jack = 3 (after I complimented

him on his cravat)

I had more hope for the rap. There was less screeching involved so at least the dogs would approve. Dev stuck **THE SUGARHILL GANG** CD in his dad's old player. At first, I found it hard to lip-synch as rapping goes at a hundred miles an hour. But Dev taught me a trick. He said if you pretend to say 'watermelon' over and over again, it looks like you know the lyrics to every song ever made. I tried it out in front of the mirror and I have to say it is very convincing.

Halfway through Jack stifled a yawn and Oli picked his nose. I wasn't put off though because I knew they would be **completely awestruck** by my finale. Dev had laid the piece of lino from Heena's Wendy House down on the floor and I took my position for the WINDMILL.

On the third spin I caught my foot on the bedside cabinet and knocked it over, along with everything on it. I went to clear it up but Agung said 'No, keep dance!'

So I carried on. I am glad I did, as the marks were a remarkable improvement on the last:

In the absence of a gorgeous assistant, Dev brought on my magic box for the last act. I asked the judges to each choose an item from the room. Jack chose a pen, Oli chose a watch and Agung pointed to a half-eaten Cup Noodle on the windowsill. I told him I couldn't use it as it was full of soup and bits of noodle and would stain his antique Oriental rug if spilled. He didn't understand a word of course. I chose an apple for him instead. I slid off the lid, placed the objects inside the box and opened the lid again to show them they had gone. Everyone was amazed. I got five out of five from all three judges – outstanding!

As I went to fist bump Dev, I smelled burning. It was coming from a smouldering pile of newspapers stacked against the wall. I prodded the pile of papers with Agung's walking stick and flames shot up!

'OH MY GOD, FIRE!' I shouted.

I picked up the nearest wet thing I could find

and chucked it at the flames. Oli got in the way and ended up being covered in Agung's half eaten Cup Noodle that I'd grabbed off the windowsill. Then Mam and Dad burst in.

'We smelled smo—' said Dad, stopping to cough and gawp at Oli dripping in noodles.

'WHAT THE HELL'S GONE ON HERE?!' yelled Mam. I thought her eyes would pop out of her head.

'I'll get water!' said Dad, running off to fetch a bucket.

After the fire had been put out and calm was restored, we found the cause. It was from a burning joss stick on top of the bedside cabinet

I'd kicked over. Thankfully there wasn't much damage. Just lingering smoke and a charred **BAMBOO GARDEN** Chinese takeaway calendar from 2003.

How to put out a fire

Bucket of water

Fire

Cup of noodles

Not a fire

121

After we cleaned up and put the furniture back, Dev said, 'That magic trick was awesomesauceness. But it needs something extra.'

'I GOT THREE FIVES, WHAT MORE DO YOU WANT?' I said.

Dev did a pirouette, flung open his arms and trilled, **'WOW FACTOR!'**

He is more over the top than a boiling milk pan, that lad. I looked out of the window and saw Oli feeding Hulk the noodles that were stuck in his hair.

'What about . . . I make Oli's guinea pig disappear?' I said.

Dev gasped melodramatically and squealed, **'Genius!'**

Then he looked concerned and said, 'Is it all right putting a live animal in the box though?'

'Yeah, I just have to make sure I catch him extra safely at the bottom,' I replied, confidently.

'How will you get Oli to agree? You just **splattered** him with noodle juice.'

'Leave it to me,' I replied, tapping my forehead.

I went outside to talk to Oli. Hulk was nibbling away like mad on the noodles.

I said, 'Looks like he's having the best time of his life.'

'Unlike me,' replied Oli, peeling a stray noodle from his eyebrow.

I quickly changed the subject.

'Has Mam got you that new **Luke Skywalker** doll yet?'

Oli frowned and said, 'I'm getting it for my birthday next month. And it's **NOT A DOLL**, it's an **ACTION FIGURE**!'

'I can get it for you loads sooner if you don't want to wait that long.'

'OK, what's the catch?' he said.

He is not as dumb as he looks sometimes. I told him that I would take him into town next weekend and get him the roving-eyed, realistic-haired **Luke Skywalker** if he would let me use the beady-eyed, spindly-haired Hulk as a magic prop. He went silent for a second and I thought he was going to scream for Mam. But he grinned and said, 'OK then!'

YESSS!

My magic act was going to be a sensation!

Saturday

The following Saturday Dev and I spent the morning rehearsing the magic trick in his garden. Dev made a special, showbiz accessory for Hulk but Hulk refused to co-operate until we took it off. He doesn't like **cherry pink, taffeta bow ties**. I don't blame him. I thought it would be difficult getting Hulk in and out of the box without scaring him but he seemed to enjoy the attention. It is miles better than being stuck in a hutch being fed manky noodles out of Oli's hair, that's for sure.

Just as I was draping a cloth over the closed box, we heard sniggering. I looked over the fence and found **EVIL TWINS** crouched behind it! They had squeezed through the gap in the fence into Mr Pike's garden and had been watching us the whole time. They soon scarpered when we told them Mr Pike was coming out with a big stick.

HA HA!

After lunch, me and Dev took Oli into town to buy him his new **Luke Skywalker** action figure. It was going to cost me my birthday money from Uncle Jim and Aunt Tanya put together. But I thought it was a fair swap for the use of a live guinea pig.

Cruckshank's Toy Shop only had one latest model **Luke Skywalker** left on the shelf. Lucky for Oli. I don't think I could have been bothered to make the trip in again just to buy a silly doll. After a quick calculation I worked out I would get precisely one pence change from my two crisp ten-pound notes – practically **daylight robbery**! The shop assistant (or Malcom as it said on his name badge) got Luke out of the box to demonstrate. He got way too excited about jointed limbs for a man in his mid-fifties. While him and Oli chatted, me and Dev looked around the shop until we ran out of things to sniff and prod. When we returned they were still at it so I fluttered my money impatiently at him.

'Oh, yes that'll be nineteen pounds ninety-nine then,' said Malcom, hurrying across to the till.

He put Luke in a bag and ceremoniously handed me the one pence change. I tried not to weep as I put it in the charity box on the counter and apologised to the photo of the golden Labrador dog for the blind on the front of it while I did so.

We'd only been in Cruckshank's for twenty minutes but it felt like an hour! Time sure crawls by in the company of Malcom. It was too early to head home. **EVIL TWINS** would still be at our house chopping off flower heads with a cricket bat or running over slugs with their tricycles. We went to the café and Dev got us chips for lunch. At a quarter to one, we caught the bus. Back home we discovered that the twins hadn't left yet. Apparently, Mr Tatlock was stuck at work and wasn't coming to collect them for at least another hour.

UGH.

We went into the garden to check on Hulk and found he wasn't in his hutch.

'Ah, he'll be asleep inside his wooden house,' said Oli, opening up the latch. He put his hand in and lifted the lid of the house. It was empty inside! **'OH NO, HE'S GONE!'**

said Oli. He scrabbled around in the hay with his hand. Then he looked under a bunch of shredded paper, searched in the food bowl, and peered under a lone sunflower seed. (He was quite desperate).

Where to find a missing guinea pig

Under shredded paper? Perhaps.

In the food bowl? Maybe.

HULK

Under lone seed? Don't be daft.

In a pack of buns? Shut up already.

'He was here this morning when I filled his water bottle,' said Oli. 'I'm going to be so in trouble with school.'

I remembered catching the twins spying on us through Mr Pike's fence this morning. I bet they saw what we were up to and decided to **sabotage** my trick by hiding Hulk. That is exactly the sort of thing they would do. They were seeking **revenge** for getting Ted's hair caught in my handheld fan and for Tod having to wear my puke-stained waistcoat to a party.

I cornered them by the shed and demanded to know where Hulk was. They stared at me blankly. 'Tell me what you've done with him or there'll be **TROUBLE**,' I said, with my best menacing expression. They sniggered and shrugged. It is shocking how they are only three and a half and already have the sophisticated minds of criminals. We split up to search. Dev in the garden, Oli and me in the house. Apart from mistaking a rolled-up flannel, a sock and a brioche bun for the lousy rodent, there was no sign of him anywhere. After half an hour we confronted the twins again. When they refused to own up, I opened Dad's shed, prodded them inside and double-padlocked the door shut.

'You're not coming out until you **CONFESS**!' I said, sticking my head next to the door so they could hear.

'Will they be OK in there?' said Oli.

I said, 'As long as they don't know how to use the chainsaw.'

'Come on, let's leave them to stew until they're ready to tell us **the truth**,' said Dev.

And dont touch anything while you're in there!

I put the shed keys on the hook in the hallway and we went upstairs to continue our hunt. We forgot all about it though when we found an old game of Dad's called **KERPLUNK** shoved on a high shelf. After two games, which I won **(YES! ANOTHER TALENT PERHAPS?)**, the doorbell rang. I heard Mr Tatlock talking to Mam. I got distracted and stabbed Oli in the ear with my Kerplunk stick.

'Owww!' he hissed.

'Shhh . . . Mr Tatlock's here and **EVIL TWINS** are still locked in the shed!' I whisper-shouted.

Then Mam yelled up the stairs.

'Are Ted and Tod up there, you lot?'

'What are we going to do?' said Oli.

'I'll get them out of the shed while you distract my mam and Mr Tatlock,' I said to Dev.

I was hoping Dev's expert acting skills would save us. We ventured downstairs, trying to look normal. I said, 'They're in the garden, Mr Tatlock, I'll just go get them for you.'

Mam looked confused. 'But I just looked in the gar—'

Dev jumped in.

'Mrs Yip, your biceps are looking buff, and Mr Tatlock, I love your crimson tie, the colour matches your eyes. Hey, have you seen this?'

Then Dev started doing some crazy tap dance routine while I took the shed keys off the hook and sprinted outside. I was half expecting them to be passed out from lack of oxygen or something, but as I opened the door, the twins came barging past, screaming and flailing their arms in the air.

'**Daddy, Daddy,**' they cried, tugging their dad's sleeve. '**She BAD girl!**' They pointed at me like I was the evil one, even though it was them that had let Hulk out of his hutch in the first place! To be fair, there wasn't certain evidence yet, but who else could it possibly have been?

Mr Tatlock ruffled **EVIL TWINS**' hair. 'Well, not everyone can be good little angels like you, can they?' he laughed.

138

I think Mr Tatlock needs a break from work. The stress is addling his brain! Seems like we got away with it, anyway. As they were leaving I stood on the doorstep to make sure they were indeed making their way off our property, into

Mr Tatlock's car and about to drive far, far away. Well, only two miles across town, but that is enough as far as I am concerned.

I was about to shut the door when Dad came through the gate carrying a bunch of random skip finds. **Plunkthorpe Council** have commissioned him to make a centrepiece sculpture for the roundabout in town. He was dead pleased when he found out. Let's hope he never finds out about EVIL TWINS being locked in his shed!

Jack and Kayla were right behind him. Jack had a new book under his arm by Charles Dickens called *Great Expectations*. He is expecting **A LOT** if he thinks his relationship with Kayla will be anything other than nerdy book club pal. He has got **no chance**. I have seen her share a satsuma with Scott Sandvick and he plays centre forward for Plunkthorpe's Youth Football Team.

Sunday

Hulk has been missing for a whole day. I double checked his hutch this morning just in case he had come back. He hadn't, but what I did find was crucial evidence! When I looked closer I found Evil Twin-sized jammy fingerprints all over the hutch. So it **WAS** them that had let him out! I showed Oli but he was more concerned about getting told off by his school. I told him not to worry as I am sure they wouldn't want that mangy old thing back scaring all the kids.

I haven't told Mam and Dad yet as they will most likely have a different view altogether about **losing** school property. They won't be happy at all, knowing it was their responsibility as parents to supervise Oli's pet handling. Oli has been ordered not to say anything to them either. Sundays are their rest days when Mam likes to do a seven-mile run followed by one hundred press-ups and Dad likes to construct some monumental feat of engineering in his shed.

In the meantime, if Hulk turns up, we can pretend he has only just escaped and act surprised. That's if **EVIL TWINS** aren't holding him hostage somewhere. We tried to keep the secret from Jack too but he got suspicious when he caught me waving a courgette around inside the cupboard under the stairs. I told him it was an ancient witchcraft ritual to ward off spirits but he didn't believe me. Then Oli came over and blurted out, 'Those cucumbery things give Hulk diarrhea!' which gave the whole game away.

BRILLIANT.

They make his poo go all runny!

Jack demanded to know what was going on so I had to tell him everything. I couldn't think of any other excuses as to why I was waving a courgette around otherwise.

I described how I was going to use Hulk for my magic trick at the variety show and how **EVIL TWINS** had let him escape. 'It was my job to make Hulk disappear, not theirs!' I told Jack they were trying to sabotage my plans and had either kidnapped Hulk and were holding him hostage or just let him run free to get mauled to death by **FUZZFACE**.

'Nah, he's more likely to get pecked to death by crows,' he said.

Oli started blubbing so I assured him it

wouldn't come to that. Crows wouldn't waste their time on anything so scrawny.

I asked Jack if he would assist in our search and to my surprise he agreed. Pre-book club, he would have **laughed in my face**, blabbed to our parents and headed straight to his bedroom for a round of **Ninja Banana 2** on his computer like a typical moody teenager. Instead he was incredibly mature and took over the proceedings with great **enthusiasm and leadership**. I expect that is the effect wearing a cravat has on you.

We had already looked for Hulk around the house. Our next step was to extend our search out into the neighbourhood. Oli was instructed to stay on guard at home in case he turned up there. Me and Jack went and called on Dev to help us. It felt logical to start in our street and work our way out, but for some reason Jack insisted we start two streets away.

HOOLIGANS!

We were standing around arguing about this, when we heard banging. Mr Pike was at his living-room window, waving his fist at us. That man should book himself a mini spa break and relax for a while. It must be exhausting gawping out of the window all the time. We decided Jack's idea was best after all. The last thing we wanted was

Mr Pike knowing we had another animal on the loose. Not that guinea pigs cause much damage. All they do is sit around *twitching* their noses and *munching* lettuce all day. If reincarnation exists I would like to come back as a guinea pig. At least there wouldn't be all these complications to deal with!

It is very posh two streets down. The houses are detached and they all have double garages and hanging baskets. Our house is semi-detached and on the edge of a rough council estate. It gave me a bit of a complex. We tried not to attract too much **attention** as we traipsed down the street but it is hard to avoid looking **suspicious** when you're stopping to rummage under everyone's shrubbery. It was a good job Jack had his cravat on, it made us look more respectable.

One lady, who was weeding her borders, got such a fright when she saw us pop up under her hedge, she ran off and got her wig caught on a holly bush. Dev came around the corner, spotted it and shouted: 'I found Hulk!' Before I could stop him, he grabbed the wig, and **SCREAMED** when he realised what it was. And I thought Agung was short-sighted!

The lady peeked at us, terrified, through a gap in the curtains inside her house. We apologised and made a point of placing the wig carefully back on the holly bush as we stage-smiled and slipped away.

Halfway down the street Jack came to an abrupt stop outside number fifty-five.

'Hulk!' he shouted, loudly. 'HULK!'

We were grateful that he was putting in so much effort, but this area was prim and proper, we couldn't go around **bellowing like louts**. A moment later, the door opened. I thought we were in trouble but then Kayla Digby emerged.

'Hi Jack, what are you doing here?' she asked. 'What's with all the shouting?'

'Oh, I'm er . . . just saving another helpless creature,' he answered, trying to be suave.

Jack is a helpless creature.

'What kind of animal?' asked Kayla, looking concerned.

'My little brother's guinea pig, Hulk. He's . . . he's **gone missing**,' said Jack, wiping an invisible tear from his face. I should tell him to enrol in Dev's drama club.

'Oh, how awful! Shall we look in my garden?' Kayla said.

And before she could open the gate, Jack had lifted the latch and was through it like a shot. Then they both went **scrabbling** in the bushes together. No wonder Jack was so eager to help, he just wanted an excuse to go past

Kayla's house and pretend to be an **ANIMAL RESCUE HERO** again. What a chump! I had to hope Kayla's kitten Munchikins hadn't mauled Hulk to death.

Me and Dev continued the search. We got as far as Dev's drama club. As we approached, we saw that all the blinds were drawn and there was a sign on the door which read:

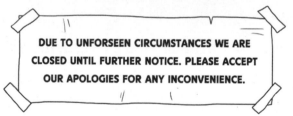

DUE TO UNFORSEEN CIRCUMSTANCES WE ARE CLOSED UNTIL FURTHER NOTICE. PLEASE ACCEPT OUR APOLOGIES FOR ANY INCONVENIENCE.

'I didn't know your club was shut already!' I said.

'Neither did I!' he cried. 'Where are we going to hold the show now?'

He kicked the wall and howled in pain.

It was a bad day so far. No Hulk, no drama club and a potentially broken foot.

'Don't worry, we'll think of something,' I said, thinking of literally nothing.

Dev kicked the wall again. He didn't care if he broke all his toes. There was no more club to tap dance in anyway. He was dead upset. I know, because I offered to buy him a packet of pickled onion **CROCODILE CRUNCHIES** when we went past the shop and he refused. The only time he has ever refused **CROCODILE CRUNCHIES** was when he had gastroenteritis. He was on liquids and had to be within dashing distance of a toilet for three days.

1 If tempted to kick a wall... ...tie a cushion around the foot first, to soften the blow.

2 Eat required amount of pickled onion Crocodile Crunchies until angry feeling disappears.

When I got back Oli was sat in the garden with Agung. He told Dad he was out there helping Agung look for the **Flaming Lycheebill** while secretly on the lookout for Hulk.

'Any joy?' I asked.

'Well if you call "joy" being taught how to say "binoculars" in Chinese for the last hour, then yes,' he answered moodily.

Tuesday - Hulk still missing

Hulk has been missing for three days. He is so fragile and delicate that I am wondering if he's been whisked off by one of those mini tornados you sometimes get. He could well be on a very nice beach somewhere in Devon right now . . . or stuck up a pylon.

Dev has perked up since Sunday. I knew, because he was wearing his beret at school break time. He only puts it on when he is in a good mood. He had an idea for his performance for the variety show. He didn't tell me what it was though; it is **top secret**. He and other members of the drama club have been to Miss Gabb's cramped town centre flat to rehearse. Apparently, her neighbours complained about over-extravagantly dressed people **flouncing** in and out, and awful show tunes blasting from her window. They don't like excitement much.

Mrs Sharma came round to tell us about an open evening at the care home she works at. It's tomorrow. She is asking people to donate homemade cakes. I have never made one in my life but I have eaten an impressive amount. (Including the time I accidentally took a bite out of a 'cake' of soap, thinking it was cheese). So far, my cooking skills include:

1. Frying an omelette which stuck to Dad's wok like a barnacle. He couldn't save it so he turned it into a tadpole pond (the wok, not the omelette).

If you ever run out of glue, just use omelette

I'm rich beyond my wildest dreams!

2. Baking a jacket potato in the microwave so long it became fossilised. I took it to school and convinced Ged that it was a dinosaur egg. He stole it off me and showed it to Mr Claypot the geography teacher who gave him detention for wasting his time. Ged's had it in for me ever since.

161

UFO ⟶
(Unidentified Frazzled Object)

3. Cooking a pizza in the oven but forgetting to take off the plastic wrapper. It set off the smoke alarm and Mam had to take it out of the oven with a shovel and frisbee it outside. It landed in Mr Pike's garden and he came out and stared at the sky in a confused manner for ages.

But I've never made a cake. I could be **BRILLIANT**, for all I know! Even better than I am at magic. Although until Hulk turns up, I can't do my act, so technically I am still without a talent. Mam was pleased I offered to bake because it meant she didn't have to do it and could finish grouting the bathroom tiles instead.

Dev helped me make the cake. We couldn't agree what type to make so we wrote down all the cakes known to humankind, cut the paper into strips, folded them and put them in a bowl. It was the most dedicated piece of homework I have done since drawing a diagram of the life cycle of a fruit fly last term. We got Oli to pick out a slip and read it.

'**Chocolate meringue Mont Blanc cake,**' he announced, getting the French bit all wrong.

I went and looked in the cupboard.

'We don't have any chocolate,' I said.

'Probably cos you ate it all,' snorted Dev.

Oli rummaged for another slip.

'Coconut and passion fruit mouse cake.'

'Don't you mean *mousse*?' said Dev.

'IT SAYS MOUSE HERE,' Oli argued, stabbing at the piece of paper.

I looked at the paper.

'Mousse,' I repeated.

'OK, OK! YOU NEVER SAID IT WAS SCOTTISH!' he yelled, storming off.

I looked in the cupboard again.

'We don't have coconut or passion fruit,' I informed Dev.

'Or mouse, presumably,' said Dev.

Eventually we found the ingredients to make a **Victoria sponge**. It was only after putting the mix in the oven that we realised we didn't have any jam to go in the middle. I persuaded Dev to come with me to the shop, as I was terrified of bumping into Ged after last time. Dev was worried the cake might burn but the shop was only five minutes away. They only had luxury conserve left and it was double the price. Just for a gingham cloth lid – **OUTRAGEOUS**! We couldn't afford it, so we trekked to the big supermarket on the main road. When we got to the till there was a pensioner in front of us counting out three pounds sixty-seven in coppers. This always happens when you are in a hurry.

When we got back, we were fifteen minutes late. Mam was frisbeeing our burned cake out into the garden. She is getting good at frisbeeing incinerated food about.

'Can you two stop SETTING FIRE TO EVERYTHING?!' she said, smearing charcoal off her face.

'Sorry, Mrs Yip, we had to get jam,' said Dev.

'We've got jam!' she said, stomping into the kitchen. She opened the far cupboard, which was full of jars in every conceivable flavour. 'They're Agung's,' she said. 'He's a secret hoarder.'

GREAT.

I thought we could rescue the burned cake but it had smashed into a zillion crumbs. (Maybe the smell of them will entice Hulk back?) Thankfully we had enough ingredients to make another. Halfway through we got distracted by Agung's immense jam collection. I noticed the hot chilli jam jars were almost empty. He loves spicy food. When we turned around Agung was standing at the table stirring our cake mix. It was very thoughtful of him. He stuck his finger in, had a taste and gave us a thumbs up. **'VERY GOOD,'** he said. I am pleased that our mix met his approval.

Dev set the timer on his watch so that we could take the cake out of the oven on time. It looked superb when it was done.

Jack strolled in, wearing a turtleneck jumper and carrying a pile of books under his arm. I keep thinking he has been abducted by aliens and replaced by a second-rate nerd.

'**Wonderful aroma,**' he said, sticking his spotty face way too near my precious cake cooling on the rack.

'It's not for you,' I said.

'Hey, chill, Nut. Merely inspecting,' he said, in a weird, floaty voice. Then he sauntered off, trying to look cool.

'What's wrong with him?' said Dev.

'**Kayla Digby,**' I answered, shaking my head in a sorry way.

Then Oli bounded in.

'Any sign of Hulk?' he asked.

'Not yet, I'm afraid,' I said, trying not to think of him stuck up a pylon somewhere.

'We'll have to tell Mam and Dad then,' said Oli.

'NO!' I screeched.

We'd left it far too late to tell them now, they would go spare! I promised him a slice of cake when it was finished and that shut him up.

'Your parents will find out, you know,' said Dev.

'I'm sure he'll show up soon,' I said. 'Let's just keep looking.'

I tried to take my mind off it by admiring my exquisite **Victoria sponge**. That's when I realised; I didn't make it, we **BOTH** did! After all that, I still don't have a talent I can call my own.

UGH.

I could have made another one by myself, but to be honest I was fed up of cake by then and Mam was fed up of chucking my burned food away.

The bird table has been put on the scrap heap. It took a lot to get that finished: Dad's expertise, my amateur painting skills, two ruined gardens and **FUZZFACE**'s dignity after we cut off her fur and made it look like she'd had an accident with a lawnmower.

How to give a cat a haircut

Professional groomer

Proper tools

Meewl

Incompetent amateur

Blunt hedge shears

Raaawlll!

Instead of looking for the **Flaming Lycheebill** in our garden, Agung has joined the local birdwatching club. His first trip is tomorrow. Mam has bought him a special mobile phone for people with impaired vision. It has extra-large buttons on it, including one that says 'SOS'. Dad explained to him that if he pressed it in an emergency, it would call us at home. Agung looked pleased and said he would use it to get his tea flask refilled.

Wednesday - Hulk missing, day four

I checked the cake first thing this morning. It was still untouched. I was worried Jack or Oli would have prodded it or licked some of the filling out. They can be absolute animals when it comes to scrounging around for other people's food. It helped that Mam had stored it in a locked cupboard overnight.

Mam thinks I have finally found my talent in baking. I forgot to remind her that Dev did half the work, but I didn't mind taking all the credit. Mam has put the cake in a decorative box that Dad pillaged from someone's wheelie bin. Mam was worried about germs but Dad told her he had steeped it in bleach for a week. He said it was as **clean as a whistle**. (I can't see how a whistle can be clean when it is covered with spittle half the time.) The cake looks brill. It will be the best one at the care home tonight.

Agung is off on his birdwatching trip today. He is hoping to see the **Flaming Lycheebill** at long last. Mam bought him a new Arctic puffer jacket. She worries about him catching a cold. It is spring and twenty degrees outside. He is more likely to suffer from heatstroke, padded up in all that goose down!

Agung wanted noodles in his lunchbox. Dad said they were too messy and made him char siu sandwiches instead. Agung was chuffed with his Chinese version of a ham sandwich. Dad also made Agung a full flask of tea and told him that under no circumstances was he to use the SOS button on his phone for refills. Agung also has a new spectacles holder. It hangs around his neck so that he can't lose them. The last thing he wants is to miss the **Lycheebill** because he is emptying

Matching footwear! It's a miracle!

the entire contents of his bag in order to find his glasses . . . and getting heatstroke while he's at it!

After school I went to watch telly in Agung's room. He wasn't back from his trip yet. I thought it would be nice for him to see the **Lycheebill** and be reminded of his homeland. Dad said Agung misses Hong Kong and wants to plan a trip back. Mam pointed out he has enough trouble getting in and out of the bath with his sciatica, never mind surviving a non-stop, fourteen-hour flight.

I went to find Oli, who was in our room scribbling something in his sketchpad.

'What's that?' I said.

'I'm making "LOST" posters to put up for Hulk,' he said.

'No, you don't need to,' I said, in a panic.

'But I'll get into trouble with the school, and so will Mam and Dad, and you're not doing anything about it!' he whined, bolting for the door.

I tried to stop him but he dodged me and thundered downstairs.

'MAAAAAAAAM!'

I raced after the blabbermouth. Mam was in the kitchen, on her mobile. She gestured at him to shush. She looked very worried. When she hung up she said, 'I knew it! That was the birdwatching guide. Agung's gone missing and they've sent out a search party!'

'Oooh, I like **PARTIES**!' Oli squealed.

It doesn't take much for Oli to forget about the **tragedy** of his missing pet.

Mam said, 'Why hasn't he used the emergency SOS button on his phone to call us?'

'Don't worry, he's probably having a nice picnic on his own somewhere,' I said.

'He'll get a nice surprise when the **PARTY** turns up!' said Oli.

He'll get that, all right.

'At least he packed his furry hat,' said Mam. 'That'll keep him warm if he's stranded out for too long.'

Furry hat?

I'm sure Agung doesn't have a furry hat.

OH NO.

If he doesn't have a furry hat, then there's only one other thing it could be . . . HULK!

He must have picked up the guinea pig by mistake! Only yesterday I found Agung signing Mr Chan's birthday card with a runner bean.

His eyesight is getting atrocious. I figured that after **EVIL TWINS** let Hulk out, he must have wandered into Agung's room, survived on leftover Cup Noodles for a few days, then passed out from the joss stick fumes. Agung must have seen him lying there motionless and mistook him for a hat. Yes, that's it!

How lost guinea pigs survive in the wild

Scavenge discarded noodles

Avoid passing out in joss stick fumes

HAT SHOP

Avoid being mistaken for a hat

Call the Society for Protection of Lost Rodents from emergency phone

SPOLR

Mam called Dad at work to tell him what happened. She got in the car and because Jack wasn't back from his after-school science club to look after us **(LOOK AFTER US? HA!)**, me and Oli had to go with her. Good job really as I had to rescue Hulk from Agung's bag before he suffocated, or got manhandled to death if Agung decided to wear him. Try explaining **that** to the RSPCA!

The birdwatching club hadn't gone far. Just to the woods on the edge of town. Mam parked in the high street and we went to check the park. We thought that by some miracle, Agung might have found his way there and was happily chucking char siu sandwiches at the logs floating in the pond. He wasn't there. Next stop was the **BAMBOO GARDEN** Chinese takeaway.

Mr and Mrs Chan were in the kitchen. We thought they'd already heard the news of Agung's disappearance, as both of them had tears streaming down their faces. But then I noticed the thirteen tonnes of onions they were chopping. They got worried when we told them, but strangely, Mrs Chan seemed to think that cooking us a **five-course banquet** would help. We stood there for at least twenty minutes while she rustled up a special chow mein, curry chicken, sweet and sour pork and several rounds of prawns on toast to take home with us. Mam was too polite to remind her we were in the **middle of a crisis**. Personally I was delighted we had popped in there. Prawns on toast is one of my favourites. Mr Chan said he would call us if Agung made an appearance.

We got back in the car and continued the search. I seemed to be spending a lot of time looking for **doddery old creatures** lately. We drove past Miss Gabb's flat. I saw Dev coming out dressed in a **furry** outfit. He obviously hadn't been keeping an eye on the weather forecast either! I waved, but he didn't see me. As we turned into the road towards the woods, Mam's mobile phone rang. She passed it over to me and I answered.

'Hello?' I said.

'It's Eileen from **Plunkthorpe Birders**,' said the voice. 'We've found Mr Yip. Not to worry, he's fine.'

'They've found him,' I said to Mam.

185

Mam looked up at the car ceiling and mouthed something that looked vaguely like a swear word.

We pulled up at the birdwatching club's meeting point. There was a crowd of people wearing khaki gilets and cargo trousers. There was no mistaking them. Agung was sitting on a bench in the middle, sipping his tea without a care in the world. He didn't have his hat on, so Hulk must have still been in his bag.

'Here he is,' said Eileen. 'We found him trying to retrieve a crisp packet out of a buddleia bush by the golf course. I think he thought it was the **Lycheebill**. It was blowing away in the wind but he kept after it.'

Agung must have forgotten to put his specs on, even though they were around his neck.

BRILLIANT.

Mam thanked Eileen and apologised to the rest of the group for spoiling their trip. They weren't bothered. It was the **most amusement** they'd had in a long time. Compared to hiding in bushes watching boring birds all day, it must be!

I kept a close eye on Agung's bag on the journey

back. There was no sign of movement. Maybe Hulk was napping. He'd had a **tough few days**.

When we arrived home, Mam looked at her watch and slapped her forehead. She was late volunteering at the **care home open evening**. Mam didn't trust Agung to be left on his own after his little expedition and Jack still wasn't back, so Agung, Oli and I had to go with her. Just as well, as I was still hoping to free Hulk from the bag. The only problem was, how was I going to do it without anyone noticing?

I fetched my cake out of the cupboard, then we got back in the car and sped off.

Wednesday evening

Mrs Sharma was standing at the main door, welcoming people into the care home. She was delighted to see that we'd arrived with a cake, as they were fast running out. It seemed that most people had turned up for the affordably priced refreshments and the game of bingo they were putting on. (The main prize was a cut and blow dry at

Shear-Lock Combs Hairdressers in town.) No one was really interested in having a tour of the facilities with a view to moving in in their old age. Even Mr Pike turned up for a **cheap iced bun**, and he never leaves the house, the old miser.

Mrs Sharma pointed in the direction of the dining hall and told us to help Bob, the kitchen assistant, in the canteen. He was on his own, trying to manage an onslaught of tea orders from a coach-load of grey-haired bingo fiends. He was doling out a million cups of tea when we got there and couldn't boil the kettle quick enough. I have never met a man with such fear in his eyes. Like a **baby deer** surrounded by a pack of wrinkly hyenas with ill-fitting dentures.

Oli and Agung sat down at a table in the corner. I gave them some orange juice and biscuits to keep them occupied while Mam and I took over serving tea. Bob wobbled off to take an aspirin and lie down in the pantry for a bit.

Agung put his bag on the empty chair next to him. I wanted to tell him to leave it in the car boot (so I could sneak back later and rescue

Hulk). But I couldn't speak Chinese and trying to say that in sign language would have made me look like I was dancing the macarena. I didn't want to confuse Agung. He was confused enough as it was!

Oli couldn't help as I hadn't told him that I thought Hulk was in the bag. He would have scuppered my plans with his big mouth, so it was all down to me. After five thousand hours, Agung finally got up to go to the loo, leaving Oli to supervise the bag. The grey-haired bingo fiends had all been served, so now was my chance! I sloped off towards where the bag was placed. It took **ages** to get there, as people kept stopping me and asking for stupid sachets of sugar and clotted cream for their scones. I was almost

there when I felt a giant hand grab my arm. I
turned around and it was Ged Sponger!

UGH.

He was here visiting his granny.

'Oi, Yip! You in charge of cake?'

he boomed.

'Erm . . . kind of,' I squeaked back.

'Gimme some for free then,' he said.

Good job Mam wasn't there. She would have
got him in a headlock, dragged him over to the
cake and squashed his ugly face in it. Then he'd
have the whole lot for free!

I searched for Agung. He hadn't even made it out of the dining room yet because his sciatica was playing up again. There would be plenty of time to serve Ged. Then perhaps he would go away and leave me to my extremely urgent, undercover operation. I went back to the canteen and got the cake that me and Dev made out of the box. I couldn't believe we'd put all that effort in just to give the first slice away to some giant clown. I handed it over resentfully.

'THERE, GET THAT DOWN YOUR BIG FAT GOB!' I said, and stormed off.

Oli was busy making **Luke Skywalker** kung fu kick the condiments. He didn't notice as I went to unzip Agung's bag. I was just about to put my hand inside when someone shouted out, 'ARRRGGHH, IT'S BURNING!' A crowd formed in the middle of the room.

'QUICK, GET SOME WATER!' yelled Mrs Sharma.

197

I ran over with a jug. It was Ged sat at a table, clutching his throat.

'That c-cake!' he gasped, pointing at the *Victoria sponge* I gave him.

Mrs Sharma picked up the plate, sniffed the cake then ate a piece. She broke out in hysterical laughter.

'It's only got a bit of **CHILLI POWDER** in it, you wimp!' she said. 'Hmm, it's quite nice actually.'

Mrs Sharma likes her food hot. I know, because the roof of my mouth fell off after eating one of her samosas last week. But I know Ged hates spicy food ever since he refused to nick my chilli con carne at school dinner.

Mam came barging up and screeched, **'What were you thinking, putting chilli in the cake?!'**

'I didn't, honest,' I said.

We definitely hadn't put chilli in the cake. We'd followed the recipe to the letter.

Then I remembered when Agung had taken over stirring the cake mix and said he liked it. Maybe he was trying to hint that he'd added ten tonnes of chilli powder. He puts chilli sauce on all his food. He probably thinks *everyone* likes it hot!

199

Ged gulped down the whole jug of water. His face turned from fiery red to a less angry pink. When he saw me he went a **furious shade of purple** and got up out of his chair. Thankfully Mam stepped in and blocked him, so he sank back down like a wounded pup. I am in for it if he ever catches me on my own!

Everyone went back about their business when they realised it was just an overgrown, **spotty schoolboy** making a big fuss over nothing. I continued my quest for Agung's bag, when Dev walked into the room wearing a tropical print blouson with puff sleeves.

'Hey, Mads!' he shouted, waving at me.

For some reason he was carrying my magic box.

'Are you ready for a shocker?' he said.

'No thanks, I've already had two,' I said, thinking about Ged wanting to kill me and flinching at Dev's pineapple-festooned top.

He opened up the box and inside was . . .

HULK!

'I went to put the lino back in Heena's Wendy House and found him **asleep** in the corner,' said Dev. 'Remember when Graham was asleep in there and we kept the door open for him? Well, Hulk must have sneaked in after Graham left.'

I couldn't believe it! Hulk was alive and well and as normal-looking as he could be for a sickly, shabby old guinea pig. Oli was overjoyed too, because his felt-tips had started to run out after doing all those 'LOST' posters. So what was in Agung's bag? I went over, plunged my hand in and yanked out . . .

A FURRY HAT!

A furry hat

So it *was* a hat after all!

An almost identical Hulk

By then, paramedics had arrived. Someone had called the ambulance service when Ged was causing a scene. Clearly it was someone who didn't know him, otherwise they would have gladly left him choking and spluttering. The commotion had caught the attention of Mrs Bogton, the **care home supervisor**. She was showing people around when she heard the siren and rushed in to see what was happening. There was a slight panic on everyone's faces as now they weren't sure if there really was a serious incident taking place. Mrs Bogton had a quick conversation with Mrs Sharma and the ambulance crew. She hurried onto the stage and picked up the bingo microphone.

'AHEM . . . ATTENTION PLEASE! I can assure you that there has been a misunderstanding,' she started.

There were a few grumbles.

'Nothing's happened for you to **WORRY ABOUT**. Autumnal Leaves is, and will continue to be, Plunkthorpe's leading care home. A **WONDERFULLY SAFE** and **PEACEFUL** haven for all our elderly folk.'

She paused.

'However, I do have another announcement to make which is not such good news. Unfortunately Bob our bingo caller has had a **FUNNY TURN** and is unable to make it for tonight's game, so we're going to have to **CANCEL**, I'm ever so sorry . . .'

Blimey I didn't know Bob was that bad, maybe the ambulance was for him then, not Ged. There was a huge roar of disapproval from the coach-load of **grey-haired bingo fiends**. One of them even threw their half-chewed crumpet at Mrs Bogton. I felt dead sorry for her, and guilty too. After all, it was partly my fault all this happened.

Wednesday evening — showtime

There must have been about seventy people in the dining room, all on the **verge of a riot**. We couldn't have people throwing crumpets about. It was highly irresponsible. Think of all those starving pigeons begging around the bus station, not to mention the mess it would make on the carpet. Everyone needed to be **calmed down**. I wondered whether I could do the bingo calling, but I couldn't remember any bingo lingo apart from 'Droopy drawers, forty-four' and 'Dirty Gertie, number thirty'. (Because they are a bit rude and make me chuckle).

I looked at Dev for some answers and there it was, staring me in the face! Dev was here, my magic box was here and so was Hulk. What better time than now to do my **MAGIC TRICK**? It was the perfect opportunity to rehearse in front of a live crowd (if I ignored the fact that they were **furious as hell**). I had a burst of showbiz energy and leaped up onto the stage. Mrs Bogton was still standing in the middle in a state of shock, so I eased the microphone out of her trembling hand and ushered her off gently. Everyone stopped whinging about the lack of bingo and stared up at me.

'Good evening, ladies and gentlemen,' I mumbled, awkwardly.

Ged guzzled water and gave me a murderous stare.

'It's such a shame about the bingo,' I said. 'But you'll be happy to know we have something else in its place, **EVEN BETTER**!'

Dev took his place in the wings. He grinned and nodded and gave me a thumbs up.

'So please sit back, relax, and enjoy this evening's entertainment which is er . . . er . . .'

Tumbleweed blew by in my head and someone shouted from the back,

'Get off, you're rubbish!'

Dev rushed on and announced down the mike, 'Let's give it up for MAGIC MADDYYYYYYY!'

Then he shoved the box in my arms. 'Good luck!' he whispered.

GULP.

I put the box on the table behind me. It already had a tablecloth on, which was just what I needed for the illusion to work. I opened the box and circled the front of the stage to reveal Hulk.

'EEEEEEK, RAT!' a lady screamed.

Rat

Absolutely nothing like a rat

'No, it's a guinea pig. With an immaculate veterinary record, I have the papers to prove it,' I assured her.

She seemed quite satisfied with that explanation, so I carried on. Everyone was **flabbergasted** as I closed the lid, muttered some mystical nonsense and made Hulk disappear. The tablecloth did a good job shielding what was really happening behind the scenes. **Two people clapped.** Not as enthusiastically as I was expecting, but it was early days. It took Harry Houdini ten years of being shackled in a nailed-down packing crate before he got his big break. That's dedication for you.

How to escape a locked crate

1. Use a hammer
2. If that fails, use a saw
3. If that fails, cry
4. Then call for assistance — ER...HELP?

Just as I secretly opened the bottom of the box to let Hulk out, we heard barking. **Oh no! Graham was in the room!** He must have escaped from Dev's house and followed him to the care home.

213

When Hulk heard him, he panicked and squirmed out of my hands. I wonder if he'd been held captive in Heena's Wendy House by Graham during his **distressing time away**? Hulk dashed out from under the tablecloth and plopped down the steps off the stage. The secret had been revealed! No one was meant to see how my trick worked. Hulk wasn't meant to be running about either, not in his delicate state.

Oh, bumbags

WOOF!

WOOF!

WOOF!

I *chased* him around the room, dodging chairs and crawling under tables. It was like a telly **comedy sketch** but unfortunately very real. Everyone laughed their heads off, apart from a few squeamish ones who covered their eyes and lifted their feet off the floor. This was **not** going according to plan. Mrs Bogton was frantically blotting her face with a hanky. She looked as if she was going to faint. The whole thing was a **disaster**!

Dev started *CHASING* too and soon everyone was in stitches as cappuccinos got knocked over and flapjacks went **flying**. Several other people joined in the chase, including Bob, who had made a miraculous recovery after probably realising he could get fired for having vermin running around in a food-preparation area.

As Hulk ran towards us, Dev and I grabbed a tablecloth and held it at each corner, ready to catch him.

'Right, after three,' I panted. 'One, two, three!' We were just about to throw the cloth over him, but then Ged came lurching at us from nowhere.

'You've had it now, Yip!' he snarled, hands outstretched, ready to pounce on me. Panicking, we threw the cloth over Ged instead. His whole head was covered up. He couldn't see where he was going and stumbled towards the open conservatory doors. We watched, **horrified**, as he **zig-zagged** out into the garden, tripped over a gnome and fell into the ornamental fish pond. Bob jogged over and hauled him out.

I might as well have thrown myself in the pond as well. My **LIFE** wasn't worth living if Ged ever got his hands on me now.

In the meantime Mrs Sharma grabbed Graham while he was lapping Earl Grey out of a pensioner's cup. He had found the remaining *Victoria sponge*, wolfed it down and was now trying to stop his tongue from swelling up. Mam had managed to trap Hulk under a milk crate. I picked him up and put him safely back in the magic box to transport home. As I shut the lid, everybody started to clap and cheer.

Then Agung shuffled back into the room. He must have got lost as he had been gone for ages. He grinned and did a bow, clearly thinking everyone was clapping *him*. I couldn't understand why they were clapping *me* though. That was the worst performance **ever**! Everything that could have gone wrong, did go wrong. But as far as the audience was concerned it was the **best entertainment** they'd had in years. Well, I suppose Plunkthorpe isn't exactly Las Vegas.

'Smile,' said Dev, through clenched teeth.

I smiled and did a little curtsy, because I'd seen people do it on the telly to the Queen. Oli skipped over and said it was the best thing he'd seen since Agung sneezed and his trousers fell down.

Then Mam barrelled over. **'I brought you round to help, not turn the place into a complete shambles!'** she barked.

After the excitement wore off and everyone went home, Mam made me and Dev do all the clearing up as punishment. It took till nine o'clock! If I fall asleep in maths tomorrow it will be for a reason other than **SHEER TEDIUM**.

Just as we were about to leave, Mrs Bogton approached. She didn't look as grey as before. I am glad she didn't **faint** in the end as we would have had to call the ambulance back and that would have been **embarrassing**. I thought she was about to have a right go at me but instead she shook my hand!

'**CONGRATULATIONS!** I've not seen everyone have this much fun since I started work here in nineteen-seventy-nine,' she said. 'You have such great talent . . .'

YESSS! I HAVE TALENT!

'. . . as a comedian.'

COMEDIAN?!

COMEDIAN?!

I had just tried to perform the most sophisticated magic act imaginable, and she thought I was some kind of joker! When will I ever be taken seriously?

'Yes, that's right, Mrs Bogton, comedian,' replied Dev, giving me a 'Just go with it' kind of look. So my talent turned out to be the one thing I didn't want it to be! While Mrs Bogton was singing our praises, Dev told her about the variety show and how we didn't have anywhere to hold it since the drama club shut down.

'So if you want more premium entertainment like we had tonight, then why not let us perform the show here?' said Dev.

'THAT WOULD BE ABSOLUTELY MARVELLOUS!' said Mrs Bogton.

So now we have a venue, I have a talent (even though it's the wrong one), and the drama club will be saved!

Some of the care home residents gave me gifts in appreciation for an entertaining evening.

I am not sure what to do with the meat grill or foot spa, but I'm sure there's room in the cabinet trophy for a replica eighteenth-century milkmaid figurine.

Either someone's false gnashers have fallen in the box of stuff, or this is the worst gift ever!

Thursday

The next day me and Dev went to tell Miss Gabb the good news. Now she could finish rehearsals at the care home and hold the show there too. She was so **chuffed**, she did a twirl and broke an ear off a medieval pig head on a platter. Since the drama club was shut, she has had to move all the props from there to her flat for storage. She can't wait to get it all out of there again, as the stuffed Alaskan moose was taking up the whole sofa. She said, 'At least Doris downstairs will stop banging her broomstick on the ceiling. Honestly, you'd think there was something **wrong** with people tap dancing above you first thing in the morning.'

We gave Miss Gabb Mrs Bogton's number. She thanked us for finding the venue and offered us both free memberships for a year when the club reopens. Dev was dead pleased but I said I would think about it. Even though I was now a talented **COMEDIAN**, I wasn't sure if I wanted to spend the rest of my life being laughed at.

Miss Gabb decided on a date for the show. It will be in two weeks' time. My act was pretty much sorted but Dev was still rehearsing like mad. He still hasn't told me what he is doing. He wants it to be a **SURPRISE**. I don't like **SURPRISES**, especially after what happened yesterday. I am worried what will happen to Hulk after experiencing all that stress.

Saturday – Plunkthorpe Drama Club Variety Show Day

The worst has happened. Mam has banned me from using Hulk as an accessory for my magic act.

EXCELLENT.

'You know how nervy he is, he shouldn't even be out of his hutch,' she said. **HA!** Try telling that to **EVIL TWINS**, after all, it was them who let him out in the first place, I felt like saying.

The show was on in a few hours and I was prop-less! I didn't know what to do so I went to see Dev. When I told him my dilemma, he came up with a **brilliant solution**.

At half-past two, everyone filed into the care home dining room. There was a huge turnout. All the family were there, including Jack who had brought Kayla along for a 'cultural experience'. EVIL TWINS were there with their dad too.

Miss Gabb went on stage and introduced the show. Nicola Jenkins was on first with her **plate spinning**. I'd never heard of it before. Apparently her second cousin's milkman's uncle was a professional plate spinner in the 1980s and that's what inspired her. Nicola is in my art class and quite good at pottery. It will come in handy if she smashes any of the plates and needs to replace them.

A troop of Irish dancers and a ukulele player were next, then **Dynamites in Tights**. They are a brother and sister acrobatic duo who I thought were extremely brave. Not for attempting a triple twist straddle jump from the shoulders, but for wearing matching green spandex tights.

And now for the 'Human Helicopter'!

After them was **Princess Silvia Gomez Kumquat**. That is her stage name. Her real name is Maureen Snodgrass. She sang a song from the musical *Les Misérables*. It was ever so depressing. One lady started crying hysterically in the front row and had to be taken outside for air.

How to choose acts for a great variety show

Does it have crockery on sticks?

Does it have an annoying plinky plonky instrument?

Does it involve disturbingly shiny tights?

Does it include a comical-sounding fruit name?

Then it was me. My original plan was to re-enact what happened at the care home open evening. Except this time Hulk was at home recuperating. Thankfully Dev's idea was **perfect**. He got me to borrow Agung's furry hat and attached a long piece of transparent thread to it. It would be Hulk's replacement stunt double! When the false guinea pig dropped out of the bottom of the **MAGIC BOX**, Dev would pull the thread from the side of the stage, thus appearing to make it escape, and I'd pretend to chase it around.

Luckily, everything went as planned. The audience doubled up with **laughter** as I dived about trying to catch the runaway rodent. A man stood up during the clapping. I thought I was going to get a standing ovation, but he was just peeling a **midget gem** off the seat of his trousers.

When it was time for Dev's act I was ever so excited. It turned out that what he'd been rehearsing **all this time** was a mini musical about Hulk's missing days! Dev was dressed as Hulk in that furry costume I saw him in and sang about being kidnapped by EVIL TWINS (played by Dynamites in Tights). At this point I glared at the twins and they looked guilty for once. They were hoping never to be found out and now everyone in town knew their evil ways! There was also a song about living off noodles in Agung's bedroom and one about being discovered in Heena's Wendy House. It was all **very emotional**.

The show went down a storm. The audience clapped for so long Miss Gabb led us out on stage and we linked arms and did a bow. I spotted Jack and Kayla three rows from the front having a secret giggle. They had matching cravats on.

YUCK!

Miss Gabb had called the **PLUNKTHORPE DAILY BUGLE** to take pictures and write a story. The performers were interviewed and treated like minor celebrities. (I might reconsider the free annual drama club membership as I could get used to all the fuss). The journalist said the story would be on the **front page** of the newspaper tomorrow. I can't wait to see it!

Mrs Sharma, who had been in charge of ticket sales, whispered into Miss Gabb's ear. Miss Gabb whooped and announced to the room that we had raised enough to reopen the drama club! After packing up, Dad gathered everyone to get in the car, but Agung was nowhere to be found.

Mr Tatlock had seen him leaving during the plate spinning. 'I don't blame him. Even I was nodding off at that point.'

Mam's mobile rang and when she hung up she said, 'Don't worry, Agung's at Mr Chan's. They'll drop him home later.' Apparently, he had fancied noodles and wandered off to the BAMBOO GARDEN Chinese takeaway for his tea.

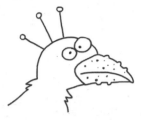

Sunday

The next morning, Dad went to the newsagent's bright and early to get the **PLUNKTHORPE DAILY BUGLE**. I even had the scissors ready to cut out the article, frame it and display it in the cabinet with the rest of the trophies.

Dad's face dropped when he handed it to me though. I looked at the front page and saw why. Instead of the variety show, it was a picture of Agung — with the **Flaming Lycheebill!**

Mr Yip pictured with the exotic 'Asian Flaming Lycheebill', so called due to its beak resembling the lumpy red skin of the tropical fruit

Dad took it over to Agung and asked how on earth it had got there. Agung put his specs on and laughed loudly when he saw it. He said something in Chinese for what seemed like an **absolute, agonising eternity**, then Dad translated. He said that yesterday, while Mr Chan was driving him home, Agung had spotted the bird on a wall. It definitely wasn't a crisp packet this time because he was wearing his specs for once!

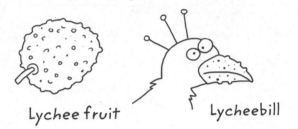

Lychee fruit   Lycheebill

Mr Chan quickly pulled over, took a picture of Agung standing in front of it and emailed the photo to the newspaper office straight away. I couldn't believe it! The front page, hijacked by my own grandad!

I turned over the front page in a huff and to my surprise, there was the drama club article taking up a whole double spread on pages

two and three — **WHOO-HOO!** Plus in the
caption above the group photo they described
me as . . .

Eeeeeeeek!

(The talented Maddy Yip) (centre right, wearing furry hat)

AT LAST! I WAS TALENTED!

And that's all that mattered.

The end